WIDOW
WALK

GERARD LASALLE

AVASTA press

Widow Walk is a work of historical fiction. Apart from some well-known actual people, events, and locales that are part of this narrative, all names, characters, businesses, organizations, places, events, and incidents are either a product of the author's imagination or are used fictitiously. Any resemblance to current events or locales, or to living persons, is entirely coincidental.

Published by Avasta Press
Seattle, WA
www.AvastaPress.com

For ordering information or special discounts for bulk purchases, please contact Avasta Press at 2400 80th Ave NW, Seattle, WA 98117, orders@avastapublishing.com.

Learn more about the author at www.GerardLaSalle.com

Design, composition, and cover design by Greenleaf Book Group LLC
Artwork by Randy Mott; Editing by Sherry Roberts; Cover photos: ©iStockphoto.com

Publisher's Cataloging-In-Publication Data
(Prepared by The Donohue Group, Inc.)
Lasalle, Gerard.
  Widow walk / Gerard Lasalle.—2nd ed.
   p. : ill., maps ; cm.
  Issued also as an ebook.

  1. Northwest, Pacific—History—19th century —Fiction. 2. United States—Territorial expansion—Fiction. 3. Culture conflict—West (U.S.)—Fiction. 4. Frontier and pioneer life —West (U.S.—Fiction. 5. Indians of North America—West (U.S.)—Fiction. 6. Historical fiction. I. Title.
PS3612.A83 W54 2013
813/.6
2012953323

ISBN 10: 0692433708
ISBN 13: 978-0692433706
Printed in the United States of America on acid-free paper

13 14 15 16 17 18   10 9 8 7 6 5 4 3 2 1

Third Edition

To the epiphany-bringers

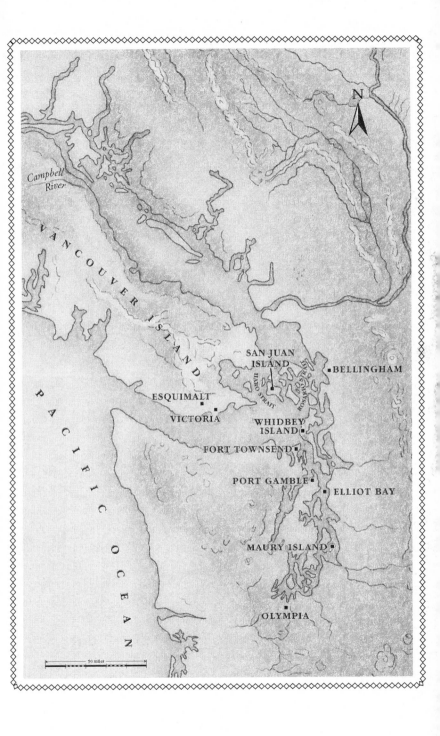

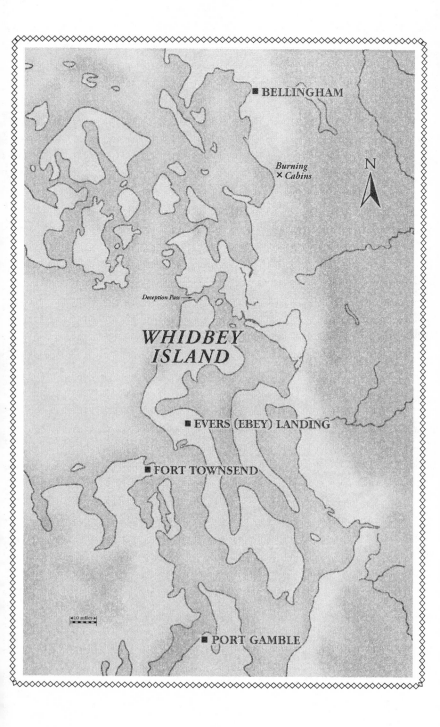

CHAPTER ONE

◇◇◇◇◇◇◇◇◇◇◇◇◇◇◇◇◇

ISAAC

The smoke was always sweet compared to what he had known in Ohio where the evergreens carried less pitch than these big red cedars and Northwest firs. As he and Sam pushed their way up the September coast from Whidbey toward Bellingham, the salty air burnreddened his cheeks, and the small fire caught in the tall trees hugging the shore in the distance wakened him fully again. The constant drizzle kept the fire from turning into a big one, he thought. Autumn five years ago had been dry enough that it took two months for the fires on the peninsula to burn out. But the trees were wet now from a steady, damp, disappointing summer, and he often wondered whether the mold he found on everything at home caused the dark green in the forest canopy too. He hadn't expected it to be so when he moved west for his life's chance. He had heard the rocky sound was clean with life and land was virginal and free—harder than in Ohio and Missouri, but in a different way. More people to mourn his losses and mark his milestones back there, but more to test himself against here. And now it was the land and the childlike natives of this region who he always seemed to be either protecting or fighting. But he had no regrets. He'd made his name here, marked it as his own.

As he watched the fire onshore, he almost forgot the weariness and ache in his shoulders and neck. Shoving off in the darkness after a long night at home became harder each time, but they had to get north quickly because he had to try the case at the Bellingham mill and get back southwest within six days for another one in Port Townsend. Not a civilian against military trial this time, but another dispute between the settlers there and a native—this one over a knifing because of cut fish nets, for God's sake. And going along the coast by canoe with Sam was the fastest way, if the weather was with them.

He hated leaving again. Emmy was fighting a fever, and he knew she might lose this pregnancy too. She hadn't seemed to take as well after the quickening this time. He had two healthy children—Sarah from another father and Jacob his own—and two recent failed pregnancies, both early losses. Emmy had kept her figure as hard as she worked, and it surprised him she had gotten sick again because she carried herself so fiercely in all she did. It surprised him that fever had caught her because she moved so fast in this world. He knew that when he returned from this adjudication chore, he'd find she'd been out of bed, filling the larder with fall berries and preserved greens, so full of fire herself. That always gave him hope. She was the home. More and more, he just tended the fire.

Sam stopped paddling, and it took Isaac, staring at Sam's back, four full strokes to notice, as full of Emmy as he was. Getting his bearings, he figured they had covered about forty-five miles, still far south of Bellingham now but passing several reef net setups. So there were Lummi nearby. Strange that the nets weren't being tended, which meant either the fishing was bad, odd for this time of year, or they'd gone ashore for some other reason. His eyes weren't any way as good as Sam's, so it took him cupping his hand to his forehead, squinting to see the source of the smoke on the beach. It wasn't the trees alone; the remains of cabins—whitewashed settler cabins—were on fire at the base of the small forest fire.

They drifted and watched for a few minutes until Sam pointed to a spot on the beach about a half mile north of the cabins. Isaac started to protest then saw what Sam was watching. It was a longboat. On the beach not far from the cabins. Medium size, high gunnels, large enough to hold fifteen or sixteen. Isaac couldn't make out the markings from here, but a raiding party, almost certainly. The boat was unattended, so that meant the cabin folk had likely fled into the forest and the raiders were hunting them. Isaac felt for his musket but kept his eyes on the longboat. Wished he'd brought more powder than what he thought he would need for hunting and bear. Wished Pickett and the federals would finally get their steamer gunboat and put a stop to this type of butchery. If the Brits had gunboats, why couldn't the Oregon territory get one for its citizens?

They made their decision. If they turned to run against the incoming tide or put up their sail to tack against the wind . . . they couldn't outrun a longboat. They had to reach shelter. Sam set the pace, fast and smooth. If they moved swiftly, they might make it to the shore undiscovered then wait for the raiding party to leave. No time for anything but hiding like the settlers, whoever they were. Isaac should have known them, being the appointed official for the region. But settlers were showing up all the time nowadays, drifting up from the goldfields in California or coming overland from Missouri and the Midwest; too many to get to know anymore. These folks had found themselves a smooth-stoned beach and built a place close to the salmon and clams. "When the tide goes out, the table is set," they'd likely heard. They had settled onto the beach and gotten lazy, typical for whites. They didn't know northern raiders had never really stopped their slaving runs. You just didn't hear about them as much because so many natives had died of measles and smallpox north of the Vancouver Islands. But the raiders hadn't changed their ways, and new settlers brought a lot of useful things with them that drew thieves out from their protected coves—Kwakiutl, Tlingit, or Haida likely. Sam would know. His tribe had to fight them all the time. Headhunters all, he'd said.

Isaac and Sam pulled up on a short spit that jutted out just far enough that a casual look up the beach wouldn't reveal them. Sam was out of the boat and up to the crest before they landed. As cautious as Sam was about everything, Isaac had never seen him scared this much, and his quiet, crouched movements told Isaac that Sam was close to panic. Faster now, Isaac secured the boat and joined Sam. They could see the longboat and part of the closest cabin, still smoldering. It was getting dark. Isaac looked behind him and saw that the little beach wouldn't give them much protection if they had to fight, and the flat between the cabins and where they hid, covered by brambles right up to the tree line, would make it difficult for him to detect anyone trying to flank their position. Sam would have seen that too. Even if they had reached the spit unobserved, if the Northerners headed out moving with the tide, they would pass right by the spit. It all depended on what they brought out of the burning forest. If their boat was full, they wouldn't stop. They would stay away from Bellingham and likely keep their heading west of Whidbey where Isaac and Emmy lived. They'd just slip back up north quietly through the small islands and up past Vancouver—if their boat was full. Still three hours until complete darkness. He would not make the trial in the time he'd promised in either case.

CHAPTER TWO

<><><><><><><><><><><><><><><><><>

EMMY

I t was already light, so she pushed herself out of bed. Too much to do every day now. Fall lingered here on Whidbey, but when rain started in October, it got cold fast, and last winter was worse than the one before. The natives talked about snow as early as October and as late as May, but the snow had never bothered her because it never lasted long. She had weathered here long enough to hate the gray, drab skies that would come soon enough, moving from warm showers to a bitter, soggy, constant drizzle, keeping her inside the small house and, with that, inside with her fears and suspended hopes. It would then settle heavily onto her, a depressing, weighty sadness, pulseless and leaden in its countenance. And that forced her this time every year to search deep down to remember the freshness of light and color, so pervasive was that gloom. By now she had learned the value of that forced exercise that would help her forbear again until spring arrived, but she still had to discipline herself better, she had decided.

Somehow, protected during her childhood by the softness and refinery of the Boston hilltop brownstones as she had been, she knew she needed to learn the seasons finally and then outlast them, keeping a strong visage in the face of it all if she were going to be the respectable wife and mother that Isaac expected.

And there were little breaks that brought hope. She knew Isaac would return with provisions from a stop in Bellingham, and more would come in right after that when her neighbor, Ben Crockett, Missy's husband, returned with his canoes stringing behind him from his trip down south. More jars and paraffin for preserves, perhaps a bolt or three of practical cloth, some cinnamon and cloves, and lots of pepper, if it lasted. So many settlers had come into the area, new provisions didn't last long before they were redistributed across three counties. And maybe something pretty—sashes or soft ribbon or even tiny pearl buttons if a British or Spanish ship or a fast one from San Francisco had been in town in the last week. She needed so much to be complete, to make this small house into a respectable home. And she wanted the baby to see some softness and color when it came into the world. She needed another girl.

Sarah was already up puttering, dawdling a bit from her outside chores. Jacob would have to be chided up again. He worked hard for a lazy five-year-old, prone to discharging his duty in spurts of blinding fury, whereas Sarah was steady and intensely stubborn, quiet and self-absorbed so that she seldom needed any attention, or so it seemed. She protected her slower little brother in a tender, defensive way that gave Emmy some reassurance that, should anything ever happen to her and Isaac, Jacob would have someone to care for him.

Emmy wondered where they got their blue eyes that made them appear as if the things they saw just disappeared inside their heads and stayed unprocessed. It had to be from their fathers' lines somewhere because she had no recollection of blue eyes on either side of her own family. She had always been told the intensity of her own brown eyes burned deeply into every person with whom she interacted, like she had the ability to disinter a person's buried emotions with a single focused stare. She had always assumed that was because she had been told as a little girl that dressing down someone with your eyes was a rude habit, and so she had taught herself to take in everything about a person without wandering her focus up, down, or around the way others did when they bothered to pay attention to something or someone. And she had always believed everything was important in its own way and therefore valuable, with bits and pieces to store away for understanding later as necessary. Everything. Isaac had said he was smitten from the first time she did that to him, but she didn't understand that because she had just been looking at his soul and she thought smitten was a funny word for anyone to use about her.

Now that Isaac was back from the inland war with the Indians, she found herself searching his soul again. He had changed, but she wasn't certain fully how yet. He seemed sadder and resigned somehow. Whatever he had seen east of the Cascades when he had led his volunteers to fight the Palouse had stooped his shoulders a bit too. Isaac came back commissioned as a militia colonel, but he had traded something precious for that rank. She knew he knew it bothered him more than it did her even. She felt it sleeping next to him and even when they had the privacy to be intimate when the children were over at his brother's home. It was in his hands and all up and down through his back. They had never been stiff before like that, before he went east. Vacant roaming now, during those private moments. And later awakening with him gone, wandering the shore on moonlit nights, coming in before dawn but up again early, throwing himself at this job or that obligation, never saying no to any task, official or neighborly. She felt alone again, more than when he had been on long trips doing his legal work; more than when she was married to Sarah's father, a rich husband she had hardly known; more than when she had been a young teenaged girl not that long ago in Boston.

Emmy understood that Isaac knew long absences were not good for the children, that she wanted him to spend more time with them. But he had put that aside because he thought Jacob was too young to accompany him, even on short trips to Olympia, and he didn't think it safe to bring Sarah on trips either, as feisty a young girl as she was, because even the friendly people were rough. Most carried some ready weapon at all times, even when using the courthouse privy.

Emmy wanted Sarah and Jacob to see New England someday, perhaps meet their grandparents before they passed on, meet cousins and aunts from both sides. But Isaac's departure for eleven months to fight Indians had stopped those plans short. He had outfitted an entire company of men, even supplying some of the poorest with shoes and weapons. The government, by the verbal oration of the territorial governor, Stevens, had promised to compensate Isaac for his patriotic advance, but no payment had come, and it had already been over a year since that bloody affair. It wasn't that they were poor. Actually, Isaac was paid very well for his legal and tax-collecting work and had been the first settler to stake claim on Whidbey—over a square mile of prime fertile farmland bordered by waterfront. He had hired hands farming it and was selling the beef and produce to the military and to every ship that came by way of Bellingham or Port Townsend. The narrow slice of land they owned controlled easy ports to both sides of the island.

Since Isaac's return, she had to share his time and stay in subservience, whether she agreed with him or not. Because of his work in Olympia and with the militia, he had become the most respected leader in the area, more so than Dr. Edwards even. But at least when Isaac was away, she had run the farm in her own way and had done quite well by it, increasing the production even without the hired hands and farmers he had taken with him to Walla Walla to fight Kamiakin on Wright's fatal expedition.

Now that Isaac was back, she had stepped to the rear as she had been taught was her duty. He had jumped right into incomplete projects like building the huge, long landing dock off their property so that deeper draft vessels could off-load without fear of grounding during all but the lowest of tides.

That project immediately increased their fortune and led to the rest of the prime property on Whidbey being claimed variously by several new neighbors, many of whom were finding a second or third chance after striking out in the gold rush that was starting to waver in San Francisco. Still, despite the prosperity and pride she had in Isaac's accomplishments, she felt like something had been taken away from her when he returned. And she resented it, not knowing whether to blame herself for not protesting his foolish risk taking, or to complain to Providence that the rewards were so greatly outweighed by the loneliness she felt on the worst of days, magnified so intensely by the dark dampness of the region. And the prosperity wasn't all that important to her in any case. She had been on both sides of the convenience it brought, so she knew she would survive without it. His absence, and her resourcefulness in raising her children in that hostile country, really had given her the reassurance that she had a wherewithal more important than any contrivances money might buy. And those who dealt with her during Isaac's absence had learned that the steel in her tiny frame had a spring-like memory.

CHAPTER THREE

◇◇◇◇◇◇◇◇◇◇◇◇◇◇◇◇◇◇◇

ANAH-NAWITKA

Hlgahlas Tatsu (Black Wind in Haida) Anah-nawitka-halo-shem, "Has No Shame," as he was called in Chinook trading jargon by tribes up and down the British Columbia coast, had been raised by his father's aging aunt. She took him on only at the insistence of a father grieving for his young wife. Anah's mother had been lost to measles in the first wave of disease that hit the Haida after Protestant missionaries passed through the Charlottes, attempting conversion and, when that failed, bartering for specimens of tribal artifacts for sale to collectors in New York and London. The Haida and the Bella Bella called the malady "Tom Dyer," after one of the sailors on the missionaries' vessels. Thousands perished along the coastal areas over a two-year period before the epidemic burned out.

Anah's only siblings, two older sisters, had been taken away by the Boston Men when his father was away one spring hunting in the far north. The American fur traders had come to the village talking about buying small black shale totems that some women and older men carved during the winter months when they had to stay in the longhouses. But instead, the traders took the pieces that had been displayed and then grabbed the two girls. Anah watched the entire event from the beach, the Bostons pulling the younger of his two screaming sisters by her hair into their boat and paddling to their big boat with sails anchored offshore. They didn't take him, as sturdy a child as he believed he was, just the girls. When his father, Little Raven, returned, he was angry. Howling like a wolf, he beat Anah every day for a week. No one ever saw the girls again, although Anah saw them in his dreams, on the beach, running away from him.

As he grew older, Anah became sullen and quick to hurt others for perceived wrongs, prone to long rages and howling violent demonstrations. By the age of twelve, he had killed two grown men in retribution raids against the Bella Coola along the inland straits off the big Island of Vancouver. Because he was tireless and accurate in his hunting and trapping skills, Anah was allowed to accompany his father and the elders in their small clan on a slaving run down into south Puget Sound, a coming-of-age honor that was not accorded other young men in that region. That caused some enmity between Anah and the young men who were not given the same privilege, but everyone already understood he was unique in a strange way that needed to be respected and, as well, given distance.

To move as a man in the longboat, one had to push the oars fast in concert with warriors seasoned to successfully chase wounded fleeing prey and outrun the lumbering ships of the Brits and Russians. Taunting the Brits by paddling ahead just out of range of their cannons, in particular, was a great coup, and the Royal Navy had never caught a longboat with any of its sailing vessels stationed in British Columbia. The Haida, masters of the tides and currents all along the inland coast, loved to tell how they outwitted the King George Men and the Bostons, just as all neighboring and distant tribes had lore about how they had outwitted the Haida. The Brits, however, simply brooded over this frustration and requisitioned for improvements in their Northwest fleet, bigger cannons and faster ships, to finally catch the insolent marauders.

Off Maury Island, on that run deep into south Puget Sound, his clan's longboats set upon a small two-masted schooner caught in a windless drift five hundred yards offshore. Anah was the first to board the hapless vessel, whose crew had been alerted to the Haida's approach by their syncopated, grunting war song. The prows of the longboats had ornate fierce clan carvings, and standing behind the big-eyed figurehead on the lead boat was the shaman of the clan, Klixuatan, dressed in bearskin and capped with a huge, monstrous, long-beaked raven mask. He stomped his spear onto the deck, blowing a whistle and singing in a high-pitched whine. The oarsmen pulled the boat forward, paddles dipping the water in synch with the stomping beat.

No shots were fired because the schooner crew carelessly

had left their powder to molder outside in a wooden bin. But, because the sound carried well across the still of the morning, they had had at least five minutes to prepare themselves for the onslaught, and a fierce knife fight ensued on deck, seven terrified men against two large converging longboats, each carrying twenty-five warriors.

Anah killed two more men that morning and took his first head as a prize, that of his biggest opponent, an orange-bearded, long-haired man with a knot braided in the Chinese style. For the first time, Anah saw the difference between the fierce, terror-filled eyes immediately before an opponent's death and the flatness and colorlessness caught in those same eyes when all life had drained away. The dead eyes on his prize were different from those of one who had simply given up living, as he had seen on his hobbled aunt the year before. He thought about how her eyes had become black holes, filled and tired and taking in no more. These eyes, however, were without color, as if the spirit released with the beheading had carried their hue away with it. After the killings, one of the longboats stayed behind to ransack, then set aflame the schooner while the second boat proceeded southward. Anah crowed his pride for hours after the killings.

Maury Island, a triangular landmass roughly three miles across, was named for William Lewis Maury, a friend and member of the surveying party of Lieutenant Charles Wilkes. Wilkes had distinguished Maury Island from the larger Vashon Island, which had been named by the surveyor George Vancouver at the end of the eighteenth century. The islands were separated from each other by a small waterway, passable during a medium tide, which led into a natural harbor bordered by each landmass. Vashon had recently been swept by a large forest fire, and the local Suquamish Indians who remained had moved their encampments onto the higher northeast bluffs of Maury, a position that presented access to the beaches below and a two-hundred-eighty-degree view of the entire sound. They could see all the way from the big mountain "Tacomat," called "Rainier" by Vancouver, up along the Cascades and the white-haired woman mountain—called "Kulshan" by the Lummi—over to Whidbey, and then westward to the sacred peaks of the Olympic Mountains.

The Suquamish watched the brief, bloody battle below. They knew about the Northerners and, for generations, had heard verbal renditions from elders who, like many tribes along the Puget Sound, also had contended with them. The Suquamish women, fearing a landing by the marauders, spread out into the forests of Maury, looking for hiding places for their children and for the settlement's few possessions, while the men of the clan, encouraged that this was a small war party moving in only two longboats, plotted an ambush. The leader of the clan, Na ma t'shata, argued that they outnumbered the raiders and had many more craft, and because their own boats were smaller than the raiders' boats, they were much more maneuverable. The smaller of the raiders' longboats had passed through the narrow channel on an outgoing tide, while the larger one lingered, its warriors busy dismembering the stricken schooner. The tidal flats between the two islands extended for almost a mile, and when the tide moved out, it did so swiftly, leaving all but the smallest of craft passing through the passage stranded and immobile for hours. An attack against the lead boat in the deep harbor by several of the Suquamish craft would overwhelm it, especially if they could hurl the large boulders they had collected for a purpose like this into the canoe of the Northerners. The tribesmen had carefully selected the stones over the past four years since the last time raiders had passed through. Anticipating a return sometime, they had conferred on each huge stone a name for incantation during the dangerous approach to the Northerners. Heaved by two men from a smaller canoe, the stones would punch holes into the bottom of the larger boat, then, from their small craft, the Suquamish would be able to spear or drown the surrounded Haida warriors. Then, Na ma t'shata predicted, they could go back and finish off the remaining immobilized warriors in the shallow channel.

Anah was in the first boat through the channel, carrying its war trophies still dripping the blood of the beheaded sailors. His father, Little Raven, had directed the warriors to head toward the south shore of the harbor, where several years before they had found a rich Suquamish village with racks of drying salmon, some metal utensils and axes, and stores of fresh water. They reached the shoals but saw that the village was gone, so they started moving into deeper water out of sight of their second boat. As they moved around a small peninsula, the Suquamish came at them, fifteen boats moving in from three sides.

Anah, seeing two warriors in one of the approaching canoes struggling to stand up with a massive stone, immediately understood the tactics being advanced. He barked to the warriors in his boat to stop paddling and instead commanded them to use the long oars to stave off the smaller canoes. As they did so, Anah impaled the severed trophy head onto a pike and pushed it into the faces of the oncoming attackers in the closest boat. Several Haida warriors leaped into the water and pulled on the gunnels of the lead Suquamish boats, which were rocking unsteadily as their occupants struggled to stand with the large stones. Three canoes tipped, including Na ma t'shata's, and the rest of the Suquamish, seeing this, broke off the attack. The Haida longboat moved back to the shoals where their other boat was wallowing. The Suquamish made no further attempts. Na ma t'shata, untouched but very dead, washed up on Maury two days later.

By the time the raiding party returned to its small village three weeks later, the thirteen-year-old Anah had acquired three more heads and a reputation for mutilation of the dead. This form of barbarism was not the custom of his clan, and it embarrassed his father. But it did not matter, for everyone understood thereafter that Anah had a brilliant dominating presence that made him special in the tactics of war and survival. Klixuatan, who had witnessed Anah's actions during the battle with the Suquamish, pronounced that the vigor of the clan was with him.

Although his aging father remained chief, Anah became the resonant leader of the Raven clan. His reputation among the numerous Haida and other tribes grew over the next seven years, rivaling the formidable tyees of the Tsimshian and coastal

Chinook tribes, whose warriors numbered in the thousands. And, because of Anah's proclivity for rape and occasional cannibalism, even the Spanish, who rarely sailed this region anymore, knew his name and steered alert in the Hecate Strait that ran between the Queen Charlotte Islands and the mainland. The Hudson's Bay Company, given exclusive domain over the area by the Crown, soon put up a bounty for Anah and raised it twice, but no one was foolish enough to bribe his way into the Charlottes to go after it. Anah's mobility on and off the Queen Charlotte Islands kept him out of the grasp of the Brits. At the same time the territorial governor, Douglas, was leading retribution excursions against dormant and well-established Nootka and Bella Coola clans, three survey expeditions out of Esquimalt, British Columbia, had set out with accompanying contingents of Royal Marines, expressly dispatched for the additional task, should the opportunity present itself, of capturing and hanging Anah. Each time, though, he and his most loyal accomplices had enough forewarning from Tlingit allies along the coast to move out of reach, abandoning villages and then taking new ones if the Brits found their winter encampments. Anah's elusiveness made a mockery of the Brits' efforts, even raiding the Tsimshian tribes in adjoining areas of the newly established Fort Simpson.

Slaving was profitable for Anah, more so than the pickings from ravaged Qualicum and Tsimshian villages, and he found ready buyers for his healthier captives from the Russians and even from a few ships venturing in from south of Oregon. As the fur trade died out by midcentury and increased pressure was brought to bear by the Brits against slavery, Anah learned the value of selling women for purposes other than labor. And his personal appetite was voracious. It was rumored that he kept several women, fair and dark-skinned, red- and raven-haired, in his own entourage. Few slaves sold by his clan escaped his mark, especially the young women and boys.

In the twenty-fourth year of his life, Anah traveled with his father and a huge raiding party—composed of several Haida, Tlingit, and Skidegate clans—far, far south along the coast into northern California. When they returned, they had over one hundred captives: young women, children, and a few healthy male teens, many of whom had fair hair and complexions. They had been snatched in quick raids on six peaceful, unprepared Umpaqua and white coastal settlements between the Rogue River and Mendocino. Anah kept young Scandinavian twin sisters for himself, kidnap bounty from a Coos Bay emigrant settlement, and distributed half of the other captives to his followers. Anah was fascinated by the twins—not with the respectful reverence many aborigines held for such children, who were a rare occurrence among Northwest Indian tribes, but with a defiant contempt for the powers that created this anomaly. The girls, ravaged repeatedly by Anah, were both pregnant within a fortnight.

One week later, he traded the rest of the exhausted captives for a small mountable cannon and several breech-loading rifles to an enterprising Portuguese slaver, who sailed south again profitably depositing the remaining victims with buyers in Mexico and Panama. By this time, Anah had collected six wives, none of whom were Haida, and from them, twenty children. With the cannon mounted on his largest cedar canoe, he began waging war on anyone who wasn't Haida or Tlingit, attacking several villages the next year. The terror was great enough that the Qualicum and even the fierce Kwakiutl moved their longhouses far away from the shore so the distance between these dwellings and their previous location came to be called "Madman land." Still, armed as he was with his own cannon on a fleet of eleven longboats, Anah was wise enough to continually evade any confrontation with the Brit navy ships.

Three years after the raid into northern California, smallpox raced through the clan for the first time, felling half the people in the area from Queen Charlotte northward up the inland coast two hundred miles. This time, the plague was planted purposefully by an evil conspiracy of whites and local natives who would never take the blame for it. Several large chests filled with trading goods, but also carrying diseased wool blankets, were set adrift in three small boats close to the inlet of the Nass River where Anah's clan was wintering. One boat floated north across the strait into Tlingit territory, and one was discovered by a Haida woman gathering goose barnacles and seaweed. She dragged the Trojan horse two miles upriver into the camp, and within a week, the first victims fell ill. Because the telltale pustules didn't present right away, several women attended the vomiting, febrile, disease-stricken first victims and, thus exposed, carried the pox infection throughout the thirty lodges. Five of Anah's wives died, and thirteen of his children perished in two months.

Following gossip from trappers of the epidemic's devastation and betting the clan would be incapacitated, the Hudson's Bay Company sent out another expedition in March, a company of 256 soldiers and a small complement of mixed-breed bounty hunters on three fast ships to capture Anah and destroy his clan, if possible. Tlingit allies, hearing gossip about the assault from natives in Esquimalt, where the Royal Navy berthed, again alerted the Haida of the approach a few days before the ships arrived. But Anah couldn't move this time. Because so many in the tribe were too ill to evacuate, Anah sent three canoes out to confront and then flee from the approaching ships to divert them from the village. The *Eurydice*, a twelve-gun, sixth-rate ship of the line, peeled off in pursuit, but the other two larger ships, the *Constance* and the *Thetis*, dropped anchor at the mouth of the broad inlet. They set their cannon broadside to the mouth of the river to prevent any ocean escape and sent 220 of the red and green uniformed marines ashore.

Correctly anticipating the most probable landing site, Anah had prepared an enfilading ambush, a tactic he had learned watching British field maneuvers. When the marines in the first boat landed and moved onto the crest of the beach, thirty of his Haida sent a devastating volley into the heavily laden troopers, cutting all twenty of them down. The troop in the second boat did not have a chance to land and was hit by a volley from a different direction. Caught by the surf sideways, the boat overturned, spilling its wounded and dead onto the beach. The lieutenant in the third boat ordered the rowers to retreat out of distance of the Haida muskets and then signaled back to the *Thetis*.

As the wounded Brits lay dying in the surf, the *Thetis* and then the *Constance* opened up and began shelling the woods that sheltered the Haida riflemen. Trees exploded above their heads, ripping them with wood and metal shards. Anah's warriors retreated in confusion. In the bombardment by the combined twenty-two cannons from the two ships, forty men and women from the clan were wounded or killed outright. Within a half hour, British marines took the beach and disembarked the remaining 180 marines. Anah, watching them land three field cannons, decided to move his warriors beyond reach. He left the wounded to the mercy of the Brits. They gave none.

The Brits, guided by Antoine Bill, a clever Métis half-breed interpreter, passed through a huge fresh burial site of smallpox victims, saw several unburied rotting corpses in the surrounding brambles, and finally found an undefended village with over 260 ill men, women, and children infirmed in several of the smoke-filled longhouses. The Royal Marine captain of the company, Jeremy Brighton, Esq., set out a perimeter guard and ordered the marines to scuttle the huge cedar longboats and spike Anah's cannon. Then they set fire to the village. Fearing the spread of disease and rationalizing their actions as retribution for their losses and the losses of the victims of many years of brutality, the Brits stationed themselves at the single exit to every burning longhouse and shot down anyone attempting to escape, including women and children. None survived. The village and all its contents, including food supplies, were burned to the ground. The official report filed by Brighton spoke of a significant encounter, detailing the twelve dead and twenty wounded marines ambushed on the beach. He spoke of thirty Indians killed in the bombardment and numerous victims of an obvious plague "that has most certainly decimated this Haida clan's ability to wage war in the future."

From a hiding place on the beach, Anah watched and

heard the wailing in the aftermath of the terrible massacre of his infirmed tribe. He went into a howling rage, finally making his way north to find the escaped healthy survivors and the warriors in the three canoes he knew would have outrun the *Eurydice*. When he reached the rendezvous position, he learned that his last wife and his two oldest sons had been slaughtered in the bombardment. Anah's rage frightened his followers, all of whom were grieving over their own losses. In the following days, he mulled over the events and dreamed darkly, carried away by a spirit that circled the ashes of his winter village.

Anah's raiding clan had been reduced fourfold. Expecting further incursions of settlers and British soldiers, Anah knew he would need to move far out of reach, rebuild quickly, and set out to build alliances with the Tlingit and Skidegates. Because rumors had spread that the Brits had something to do with the pestilence that killed so many, within six months he had a formidable enough assembly of angry hostiles that he could start up his profitable slaving enterprise again. And then, empowered with the proceeds from that, he would seek the revenge he wanted for the killing of his sons and the rest of his people.

It was one of Anah's longboats that Isaac and Sam observed from the spit.

CHAPTER FOUR

◇◇◇◇◇◇◇◇◇◇◇◇◇◇◇◇◇◇◇◇◇

PICKETT AND INGALLS

As the swell and chop pounded the small sloop, turning his stomach into an inelegant distraction, George Edward Pickett wondered why he had let himself be talked into the trek across the strait into Victoria again. Accompanied by his friend, Rufus Ingalls, quartermaster general for the Department of Oregon, and two of his casual companions, the brothers Will and Darby McIntyre, Pickett had made the trip again in civilian garb, but this time he was immediately recognized by two of his officer counterparts in the Royal Infantry Brigade stationed in

Victoria. Despite their reassurances that he could enjoy the boomtown without exposure, by the third night, he was certain he had been saluted by a few of the drunken noncommissioned officers he passed on the streets.

Although no superior officer was likely to hear about this junket, Ingalls being exceptionally discreet, Pickett had reason to be concerned about the ill effects of nasty gossip. Despite the protection from hostiles that the fort afforded to the community, because of repeated episodes of disorderly conduct by the soldiers under his command, the Bellingham townspeople already had a substantial contempt for the military establishment stationed there. So, even unfounded rumors about the drunken or wanton behavior of the officer in charge of the outfit would make it all the more difficult for him to get the cooperation necessary for the sturdy challenge of maintaining peace between the white settlers and the natives in the region. They were always at each other's throats, each using the slightest of incidents as provocation for escalated violence.

Pickett fretted about that during the long heaving ride back south and debated whether the small pleasure he had found cavorting in the makeshift pubs was likely to do much harm to his reputation. He thought about his comportment and decided it had not been scandalous. He had learned to hold his liquor in a genteel manner as a young West Point plebe, and he had practiced that control in the lonely years after the death of his first wife and daughter while stationed in Texas several years before his commission to the North-west. Thus, the gossip in Victoria at least would not be based on any public displays of rowdiness on his part. He realized during the crossing, however, much to his chagrin, that the McIntyre brothers' antics in the main street bordellos might be confused with his own more civil behavior. At least they hadn't been arrested, but he knew they were loud and grew louder still if drinking in each other's company. He would hear about it soon enough, he decided, because gossip from Victoria and Olympia was a favorite pastime for all the citizens of the region.

Victoria had become a wild town after gold had been discovered on the Fraser River in '56, and within a few months after the find, the population had reached five thousand, swelling to become an international tent city. Within a year of the Fraser strike, thirty thousand travelers had passed through Victoria, and the town's promise of sexual favors, gambling, and instant wealth built on rampant speculation had seduced the naïve and stripped the foolish. The desperate hunger of the wayfarers passing through made it dangerous for anyone not adept at defending himself. Pickett, trained in pugilistic and knife fighting, knew he could handle himself well but kept a small six-barreled pepperbox pistol concealed in his vest nevertheless. On this trip, he'd only used it on one occasion, while into his spirits and departing from a large tavern tent. He had brushed against a surly drunkard who took offense and pulled a knife. Pickett had reached for the pistol's reassurance. Fortunately, the Brits kept good order and enough sober military presence that a constable intervened before Pickett had to put the man down.

He hadn't gone to Victoria for female companionship, despite Ingalls's prodding. He was over women for now, feeling a bitter unluckiness. The two times he had fallen in love and committed to marriage, each wife had passed on a few months after childbirth. The thought of that happening again to him, such an emotional toll with all the unmanly weeping that transpired afterward, overwhelmed him. And despite a powerful ache from his groin up to his stomach, his heart just needed peace. He could not bring himself to play undignified games without love in sight; nor could he condone the thought of paying for the discharge of his baser passions. So on this occasion he behaved as he usually did, drinking with his companions to lighten, for a bit, the duty of his office but keeping to himself mostly, a decorated knight without a Guinevere in a savage land.

A few years before this trip, in the late winter of '55 and several years after the death of his first wife, Pickett had found the person whom he considered his love of a lifetime. She was a slender thing, slight enough that his round, robust features dominated the visage of the two of them when they stood side by side so that she almost disappeared, it seemed. Perhaps that is why the quietly performed marriage between a U.S. infantry captain and an Indian teen largely went unnoticed in the Bellingham community. Or perhaps it was that Pickett normally kept to himself anyway, guarding his privacy and rarely staying at the fort he had built. In the winter of '56, within ten months of marrying his "little Indian savage," as he liked to tease her in the Chinook jargon with which they communicated, she delivered a healthy, slight-framed boy. Four months later, she died in one night from a convulsive fever that followed a fit of dyspepsia. Leaving the baby with a family living close to the home he had built for his family, Pickett wept repeatedly for days on a self-granted leave. Ingalls and other friends couldn't console him. When he returned eight weeks later, he was sober and resolute with a sense of duty that stayed with him during the remaining time he spent in the Northwest. Those who served under his command knew him to be gentle and serious, carrying a grave sense of purpose devoted to maintaining peace while following orders with enough flexibility that it was sometimes misinterpreted as permissiveness by those prone to pushing their luck.

In April of '57, Pickett received orders from the general commander of the Oregon region, William S. Harney. He was to begin making preparations to move his command. With the Oregon Treaty of 1846, a prolonged and bitter international and presidential election dispute over the U.S. and British North American borders had been resolved, it had seemed. But immediately after the signing of the treaty, Northwest and British Columbia residents found an ambiguity that established a further point of contention—the wording in the document had not named the boundary waterway to which the term "strait" referred. The Brits claimed it meant the Rosario Strait, which would have included San Juan Island with Vancouver Island as a British territory, but the Oregon territorial citizens believed it had meant the Haro Strait, which would have placed San Juan Island in U.S. possession.

Recognizing the strategic value of controlling by fort and gun the most direct pathway into the harbor of rich Puget Sound, Harney ordered Pickett to maintain the Bellingham garrison, take command of troops from Port Townsend and further south, and upon further orders establish a new position—robust fortifications on this northernmost of a chain of islands that ran down the Puget Sound as far south as Tumwater. In addition to maintaining an advantage over the British, Harney reasoned, hostile indigenous people, loosely aggregated into various tribes, occupied every one of the islands. The five thousand United States citizen settlers who had moved into the Puget Sound area over the past eight years needed protection. He knew that control of San Juan Island would be important to the success of that responsibility as well.

The Hudson's Bay Company had abandoned its outpost in Steilacoom, one hundred nautical miles south, twenty-one years earlier, but it still maintained a presence on San Juan, which was immediately across the Strait of Juan de Fuca from Vancouver, most certainly for the same strategic reasons that Harney had recognized. The establishment of the fort might likely infuriate the Brits, but Harney believed the issue needed to be resolved and had never been afraid of confrontation or controversy, whether from an enemy or a superior officer. He also knew that Captain George Pickett would discharge his duty with honor.

While in Victoria, Pickett had listened in the taverns for discussion from the Brit marines about the San Juan controversy or for any signs they were preparing for any new expeditions. But neither he nor Ingalls had heard any rumors, so he surmised that perhaps the dispute was dying down. Perhaps he would not have to move his garrison after all, he speculated. And further orders from Harney had not arrived.

As he traveled back to Bellingham on this late fall day, he noticed the waters south of Vancouver were full of life that just was not present in the Chesapeake back home. They passed hundreds of sea lions chasing salmon, and boiling pockets of dogfish furiously feeding on squid. As they neared port in Bellingham, Pickett briefly turned to Ingalls and thought about their friendship and the events of the past few days. He wondered if he had diminished Ingalls's regard for him in any way. He always worried about things like that.

Ingalls, who sat on the starboard side of the rig, had been observing Pickett staring off into the distance. He knew Pickett well and how difficult the past year had been for him. He had cajoled the young captain into this trip, hoping it would pull the man out of his doldrums. And Ingalls knew what was troubling him. He was still in mourning.

George Pickett and Rufus Ingalls had been friends since their days at West Point. Ingalls, three years older than Pickett, had the privilege of seniority and the opportunity to discipline Pickett and other plebes during the hazing that accompanied initiation to the academy. Observing the accommodating manner in which Pickett responded to the top-down pranks the upperclassmen bestowed on frightened newcomers, Rufus marked him to be a good fellow. Thereafter, he always enjoyed Pickett's company and jollity, in comparison to the stiff responses and self-important strutting of most of the other plebes. And, although Pickett's playfulness and casual attitude earned him demerits, pushing his ranking down to dead bottom in his class by the time he graduated, it made the rigidity of the environment tolerable for fellows like Rufus Ingalls, who at that time looked upon military professionalism as a secure convenience rather than a calling. Over time, he grew to admire Pickett's ability to always balance levity and abandon with a sense of gentle propriety. And Pickett never seemed to lose that sense of playfulness.

In the '46 Mexican War's battle of Chapultepec, his regard for Pickett was forever solidified after witnessing Pickett pick up the U.S. flag from a wounded colleague, the young Captain Longstreet, and, under fire from Mexican Army regulars and desperate young men from the regional Mexican military academy, climb a ladder up the bell tower of the fortress, tear down the enemy's colors, and replace it with the Stars and Stripes. That rallied the Americans and seemed to deflate the Mexicans. In the midst of the wicked fight, Pickett, still waving the flag furiously, had turned to Ingalls and winked, saying, "Some fight, eh, Rufus?"

Ingalls always remembered that. He thought about just how serious everyone had been in Mexico, seeing this as the opportunity for combat honor, overrating Santa Anna and the Mexicans, and underestimating themselves and the resolve that came from their conscious participation in the expansion of the country's borders, the destiny of a righteous nation. He thought about the days in Mexico City, after they took Churubusco, all the young men in the cantinas; the happy Pickett, sporting his new bars from the field promotion he'd received from that flourish; the flush and swell of all the stories still running through their minds. Ingalls had kept in touch with Pickett after that, and when he found himself appointed quartermaster for General Harney in Astoria, Oregon, he sought out his friend who had been assigned to establish the Bellingham fort. They sported together, Ingalls always enduring Pickett's playful teasing, and had shared a few expeditions against the more hostile natives of the region.

Ingalls had been there when Pickett met his second wife, a pretty brown thing called Morning Mist.

On that occasion just two years ago, Pickett and Ingalls had accompanied a British foray into the eastern side of the lower Hecate Strait, to observe how the Brits conducted their military business with the aborigines of that region. The territorial governor, Douglas, had arranged treaties with several clans but ultimately had abandoned any form of negotiation. Instead, he had employed the same tactic as had his British counterparts with the aborigines in New Zealand—expropriating large tracts of land as white settlers moved in. Ingalls, appalled by this practice, had nevertheless been intrigued by the interactions between the British and the Northwest natives because he had personally witnessed a distinct variation in the behaviors of the natives and wondered how they might react to such scurrilous behavior.

While stationed in Texas after the Mexican War, both he and Pickett had encountered southwestern native ferocity in the Arapahoe, Comanche, and Kiowa and had chased them across dry plains in various actions. Ingalls, later sent on as quartermaster to support Steptoe in Utah, had marveled at the difference between the scruffy, lean, and vicious Apache and the Northwest Coast Indians, who were mostly fat and docile from the ready and rich food supplies that their fishing and foraging presented to them. Both he and Pickett shared the view that on the balance, in the Northwest at least, most of the abuse went from white to red rather than the other way around.

Thus, it was not a surprise to hear that a few bands of Northwest Coast Indians approached the incursion into their territory distinctly differently than the placid aborigines from many other tribes. When he or Pickett confronted natives around Bellingham and Astoria with stories of raiding, rape, and savagery, which only served to provoke the whites into further harsh retribution, the Indians always pointed north-ward, blaming Alaskan and Russian outlaws for descending into the softer south for prey and plunder.

On that particular expedition, both men found British negotiations with the Tsimshian and Stikene, which they had come to observe, particularly interesting and ultimately dis-turbing. The aborigines they encountered seemed bewildered by the aggressiveness of the British approach to the acquisi-tion of their land on Vancouver Island. Antoine Bill, whose Suquamish tribe had no fondness for any of the northern coastal tribes, seemed to be telling the natives that their X mark on the treaty documents was simply a sign of friend-liness to the Brits, who were there only to keep order and safety for all people. But the Hudson's Bay representative was expressly stating to the interpreter that the natives would have to move from the premises if they agreed to a purchase agreement. Antoine Bill seemed to ignore that statement.

As Ingalls observed one tyee lead man after another walk up to the table to place his mark, he saw a pretty face in the crowd of onlookers staring over at them. At first, he thought she was looking at him, but then he realized she was looking directly at Pickett, who had dressed for the occasion in his uni-form, complete with epaulettes and sword. After a moment, he elbowed Pickett, who turned to see the young girl. It was Morning Mist. Ingalls recalled that Pickett seemed fixed in place, holding eye contact with the girl for almost a full minute, before blushing and turning away. She continued staring at him. She was a radiant being, no more than fifteen, Ingalls recalled. Her eyes, widely spaced on a high-cheeked symmetrical face, compelled one to look back and forth at each. And when he did so, he found she conveyed both a sadness and hope. She had a comely slim figure, and her legs were straight and well formed, unlike most of the older aborigine women and men in the region who spent so much of their time on legs folded under them. She seemed demure and modest, just like all the other native women who had not been sullied by prostitution or slavery.

Ingalls had watched the shy courtship quickly unfold in the camp that night. She spoke Chinook jargon and a few words of English. "Take me with you. Take me," were the first words she said to Pickett, and she said it in a way that Ingalls understood to go far beyond a plea for an elopement. It was spoken with the urgency of a young girl who saw the dissolution of her surroundings and feared that disintegration; a girl who saw hope, bound in a projected passion onto Pickett, in an emissary from a bizarre, new world. The intensity of the plea overpowered the lonely Pickett, Ingalls observed. After that, the shyness quickly turned into a steamy, constantly charged storm. Pickett couldn't have enough of her. Within a week, he asked her tyee father, MaNuitu 'sta, for permission to bring her as his wife to Bellingham. Ingalls knew the previous year had been Pickett's happiest. Until Morning Mist died.

Pickett glanced over at Ingalls and realized his friend had been observing him for quite a while. When their eyes met, Ingalls nodded at him and gave him a kind smile. Pickett knew the look and nodded back, was reassured his friend understood him. Thinking back over all the events they had experienced together over the past fifteen years, he knew that Ingalls, more than anyone else, would forgive him for taking the liberty of searching again for meaning on the painful events of the past twelve months. He ran them through his mind for the thousandth time as the boat neared the Bellingham harbor and the home he had built for Morning Mist. It would never be the same, he knew. It would never be the same.

CHAPTER FIVE

◇◇◇◇◇◇◇◇◇◇◇◇◇◇◇◇◇◇◇◇◇◇

ISAAC

A t first, he thought that the merciful Jesus had sent the dense fog to cover them from the Northerners, but as it established itself and crept under his summer wool, he realized it would also hide movements of a flanking attack if they had been seen earlier, so Isaac began to think it more likely to be Beelzebub's trick. The fog would also prevent them from escaping because breakers near the shore would capsize their canoe and drown them if they didn't manage to head into them straight, and they couldn't see, as thick as it was. So Sam and Isaac agreed to wait it out, risking discovery and a brutal fight with the killers.

Isaac fretted that decision. His powder was getting wet, and the thin knives he kept were for skinning and filleting, not for fighting. Sam, a slight but sturdy survivor of rival clan wars and pestilence, would be of no help if it came to a fight. Isaac knew Sam would run before he would make a stand, throwing his weapons and belongings behind him, squealing in Chinook all the way.

Isaac wouldn't run. He had seen what the worst of these aborigines did to captives. In the Palouse, he had witnessed vengeful acts and random callous cruelty by the natives—gutted men impaled, butt to tongue, on long spikes; girls and women bound then raped and sodomized repeatedly for days until they had begged to be killed; their babies dashed against the rocks. And he had seen random acts of retribution by military leaders assigned to the region, covered up in the official reports—sporadic escalating viciousness, so that at any one moment the helpless and innocent were more likely to be the victims than those who started the violence in the first place.

By comparison, all told, Isaac believed the aborigines were much more apt to let their anger rampage than were the blue-coats or the militia, usually because so many of their young men were engaged in the confrontations. But, in trekking with his company across the Snake River, he had come upon the corpses of hapless travelers, emasculated and skinned men and barely living survivors who told them the ones who seemed to enjoy giving it out most were the tribal women. While the men were gambling over their plunder, older squaws, in particular, poked, prodded, and flayed. He could never imagine a white woman doing that. He thought of the civility Emmy had brought with her to the homestead he had claimed, and how everyone on Whidbey and the military with whom she dealt in Port Townsend seemed to go out of their way to stay in favor with her. It wasn't that she was not turn-heads pretty in an unpretentious way. It was that she held her own and then some against any man. It was equanimity, present with every step she took and every word she spoke, that lent itself to every situation. He could never imagine someone like Emmy becoming so vicious.

Isaac awoke, surprised he had drifted off on this thought when he most needed to be vigilant, and damned his weakness. Then he looked over at Sam and saw that his companion had moved away from his spot. Gone. The fog had lifted Sam away, while Isaac had recklessly daydreamed. Likely hiding in the canoe. Isaac wasn't sure how much time had passed, had forgotten to wind his pocket watch, initially just fearing that the winding sound itself would alert the marauders, then just forgot about it. The watch had stopped at 2:30 a.m., and there was no sign of sunrise yet. The water had receded, so he felt higher up from its edge, but he couldn't tell how far. They had covered the canoe, turned it upside down as best they could with driftwood, digging it down into the sand so the visible line of its prow would be broken to a casual glance, camouflaged to look like drift logs. Still, he knew how sharp the raiders' eyes were and prayed the surf and chop in the morning would be sufficiently disruptive to their vision so that, when the Northerners moved out, they wouldn't be able to fix well on the little stretch of beach where he and Sam had hidden the canoe. Isaac had pulled his tan oilcloth over his shoulders in the darkness and knew he had to take it off and slip behind the camouflaged boat before sunrise. Otherwise, he would surely be seen.

The drizzle started up again, masking sounds of the surf even more than the fog had when it moved in. Isaac had covered the edge of the barrel with his thumb all night to prevent condensation from creeping down into it and dampening the powder. He kept his cartridge box close to his chest. He might get one, maybe two, poorly aimed shots off at an incoming boat if he was quick, but nothing more. And if they were attacked from land side, it would be one shot then a slashing knife fight, if he were fortunate. He would have to provoke his attackers enough that they'd want to kill him outright. Or turn his rifle back upon himself, disappointing them with his last shot.

He had thought about that way of ending it many times, when he had taken his company with Wright to the Palouse country to help the army hunt down Kamiakin. So had the other men he had brought with him. The soldiers, mostly Irish, never seemed to talk about that way of ending it. Kept to themselves mostly. But the volunteers all talked about it, constantly it seemed, pulling closer and scaring themselves to sleep under the stars, weapons held ready like he held his now. They had talked about where to stick the knife if the rifle didn't go off. They all had been spooked by what they had found on the river's edge across from the Pendleton crossing, the remains of a small wagon train of Missouri homesteaders. Just the men, propped up in poses like mannequins he had seen in San Francisco. Naked. Fingers and noses and genitals gone, cut off and eaten by the crows, or propped next to the bodies, drying to a leathery brown gristle in the heat of the July sun.

Because it was the best crossing spot on that part of the Columbia River, someone had left that scene as a fresh warning. When, following one of several trails from that scene, they had finally confronted a large group of aborigines in the Walla Walla area, Isaac was surprised at how easily discouraged the savages seemed to become after a few volleys from the soldiers and his militia. And when they discharged the eight-pounder howitzer they had pulled behind them for days, the Indians just turned and ran in every direction. Then it was a matter of hunting them down, where they were hidden in the gullies, and dispatching them one by one. Isaac and his men never found any of the kidnapped women or children, and it made him wonder whether they had punished those responsible for the massacre or whether the women had been abandoned or killed by this sorry lot. It didn't matter after what he had seen at the river. The region had to be cleared for those higher on the ladder God had created.

He had drifted again. The cold had numbed him asleep briefly earlier, and because he had been too frightened to undo his breeches to pee, he just suffered through it, offering up the pain as a small sacrifice to right things a bit with God, if this were to be his last day. But he fell asleep again and then awoke, realizing he had just let go while he lay there, pissing away any grace he had accumulated. He wondered if the Lord would forgive him for this weakness. His last moment would be disgraced, but only he and God would know, and perhaps that was the way it should be, humbled in spirit by his body after all.

God would forgive this little mistake, Isaac knew. It was the bigger sins he had visited on lesser beings that needed rectification somehow. He had taken no pleasure in the Wright expedition's most violent actions, had tried to justify it by what he had seen on the riverbank, but he had looked the other way when the pathetic beings had wept over their children. He had not spoken a word to those men in his command who had descended briefly into the same savagery they were there to put an end to, once and for all. Their vicious solution, the cruelest form of eradicating an enemy, was as bad as the problem it was supposed to correct, just more disciplined in its process than the way the savages went about it.

He sighed and that awakened him to where he was. He could see his hands now, and then he became aware of something faintly moving in from the water line, a sound over the slight lapping of the gentle surf against the rocky shore. It was moving in from the right. He pulled back the hammer on his pinfire—slowly, slowly pulling it to avoid its click on the catch; quieting his breath; tightening his eardrums; peering into the fog thinning itself with the new light. The beach had expanded with a low tide in the night, and he could just make out traces of footsteps in the sand, heading away from his position. Sam's.

It came closer now, two distinct sounds from different positions on the water that he could not yet see. Not Sam. It would take two shots. Impossible. Isaac flexed his right thigh to reassure himself that his knife was still there, hadn't fallen out in the night, a quick pull for him in a desperate, last struggle. His heart was racing, pushing his pulse into his neck, roaring in his ears, loud enough, he was certain, to give away his position. Gulls started squawking at something in the distance off to the right somewhere in the fog. And then another movement to the left, closer now, within a few yards of his position. He slowly swung his muzzle to the left, expecting that the marauder would appear and come at him in a rush, or just be standing there waiting for the fog to draw back and reveal Isaac. And that moment would be the bastard's last because Isaac would not hesitate to strike him dead. And then the sound from the right again. More distinct, cautious, water dripping off something.

Then the sun cracked through the thinning mist, and Isaac saw two brown eyes, then four. A mother and her fawn watching him on the beach. They turned and walked away, leaving hoof prints in a parallel track to those left by Sam. The gulls made a fuss again in the distance, and he could estimate how far away they were now. And then the sun came over the tallest tree on the shore and the rocks gleamed, and Isaac could see the waterline below. More wildlife sounds now—a sea lion calling for companionship and the water lapping below—reminding him he was still alive.

When enough light raked the beach, Isaac slowly placed the hammer back down and moved cautiously to hide behind the canoe. He hoped he would find Sam there, but he did not. The supplies were intact, and his powder was dry enough. He pulled a piece of salted pork and a rind of cheese and ate them quickly. Although he couldn't see much behind him because of the brambles, he could watch the beach, and as the fog melted away as quietly as it had arrived, he could see for several hundred yards. He remembered to wind his watch so at least he would know how much time had passed. Likely it was at least six. After an hour, he quickly moved back to his position by the crest of the spit to look at the beach to the south, which was finally visible in the distance. The longboat was gone. The cabins had burned to the ground, and there was detritus on the beach below.

Isaac waited for another hour, scanning the horizon up and down the waterline and into the tree line, watching for any movement. He saw from the footprints that Sam had moved off into the woods at the south end of the small beach. There was a hill beyond, and if Sam had survived his flight, he was likely watching the beach below from a safe perch. Isaac put himself in Sam's mind and tried to understand why he would have left. He hadn't expected much from Sam, so it didn't surprise him when he met those expectations. But he would kill him if he ever again showed up on Whidbey.

By ten o'clock, Isaac thought it safe enough to move down the beach to where the longboat had berthed. He kept his musket cocked and untied his side knife in its sheath. When he reached the smoking remains of the three cabins, he found broken furniture, a few overturned boxes and chests, smashed crockery, and mail-order catalogs from Chicago, all awash in the advancing tide. Two dogs lay clubbed-dead on the beach. Between the rock foundations of the second and third cabins, he found a path into the woods.

He thought of Whidbey and Emmy and Sarah and Jacob, and knew he needed to head back southwest in case the marauders had moved in that direction. He was comforted that his brother and the Crocketts were close by and his home was on the other side of the most direct route for the raiders' longboat, but it was unusual for the Northerners to appear in single boats. He knew there likely would be others or a larger group of boats somewhere in the vicinity. But he had to know what was in the woods, and if there were victims, to bury them, or at least give them a prayer that they likely hadn't had time for themselves. So he walked carefully down the path, breathing quick and shallow.

He found five men, two with bullets in their chests and bellies and three bludgeoned, their heads caved in. All were stripped naked and mutilated. And all were Negroes, likely freed or escaped slaves from the South. No women or children, except for one small boy, about seven or eight, who was cradled in one man's arms. Isaac thought of his Jacob. Would his son run to him as this boy likely had during his final moments? What would his own thoughts be as he tried to defend his boy, his family? How many of the Indians would he take down with him before he succumbed? These poor folk likely had not been armed, or at least not armed enough to leave evidence of fighting back, although the Indians seldom left their own dead at the scene of the fight. He had heard that the Indians were even more vicious against Negroes, more likely to rob them when they attempted to settle. Perhaps it was because they were easy victims who hadn't learned to defend themselves very well, or perhaps it was because they tended to live isolated from a supportive community, like the one he had established in Whidbey, where folks came together to help one another in times of need.

He pulled the bodies together in one group, a gruesome task, reminding him of some of the things he had done in eastern Washington. The woods were wet from the constant drizzle and the fires he had seen the day before all but burned out, so a funeral pyre would be useless. He began piling rocks and wood debris over the bodies to delay the depredation for a while and keep the birds away at least. That took several hours, but it was only decent. And then he set out.

As he pushed his way back across the sound in the late afternoon, he thought about the irony of the massacre, that the victims had likely escaped somehow from a life of slavery only to find death and new captivity here in the Northwest from new oppressors. He wondered whether, if left alone, they might have made a go of it in this fertile land. He was grateful for what God had given him and his family, grateful and relieved the weather had remained calm, allowing for a safe crossing—a good blessing in a dire situation. He would need to stop to rest at intervals over the nine hours it likely would take for him to cross against the tide and a mild southerly. Caught, as he was, between hope and fear, he would need to watch for any activity that might indicate a ship that could carry him or a longboat that could catch up with him. He would return with a militia detail to bury the settlers. When it was safe. But knowing somewhere out there was a longboat, likely with some new slaves, and more like it, moving down into the Puget straits, he had to get home.

"Dear Jesus, Lord, give me the strength to endure this next travail. Let me see my porch and find my bed. Watch over the children and Emmy. I will do Thy will, but give me, Lord, this one last day." He said that same prayer over and over again as he paddled slowly across the sound.

CHAPTER SIX

◇◇◇◇◇◇◇◇◇◇◇◇◇◇◇◇◇◇◇◇◇

EMMY

Her duties filled a full day and much of the evening before it was too dark to do much else than sleep, bone tired, on a hard but sufficient mattress. The big feather bed her father had sent them as a wedding gift never made it around the Horn. The clipper ship had been given up for lost. Other amenities, sent by Isaac's family across the Rockies on the Oregon passage, were abandoned with many other things by Isaac's brother, Winfield, in that horrible trek that nearly killed everyone in his party. She couldn't criticize Winfield, an amiable but emotionally labile redheaded young man, because he had arrived with himself intact, in the company of Isaac's father, Benjamen, and his new wife; his feebleminded, lame older sister, Corrine; the Crocketts; the Mastersons; and five other families, all with little remaining in the way of possessions but determined as all Providence to make their passage worth it.

They had set out in vigorous pursuit of rebuilding their lives on Whidbey on the fertile plateau Isaac had first surveyed and claimed. It was a splendid homestead, flat, with the richest soil they had ever seen and easy access to the beach. Isaac had built an unadorned but ample house, so that when the family had moved up from Olympia, their first stopping place, the children each had a bedroom, and the kitchen was large enough to accommodate six people for dinner.

Emmy was patient. She was also young enough that she understood Providence would provide for material comforts in due time, if she kept to her duties, loved her children, and obeyed her husband, although Isaac had made that very difficult many times. Loving her children was the easiest thing God had given her to do in this life. Each day was new with them, and that was how they each approached it as well, especially Sarah, who Emmy had decided was much like herself, having a natural curiosity for the big and the small. As little more than a toddler, Sarah would sit for long stretches studying the ant pile near the woodshed. And Emmy had observed her walking around and around the deck of the British steam cutter during a visit to Port Townsend, touching every knob and dial in the engine room, following the straps and levers, and only after she had found questions she could not answer by deduction did she render questions to the engineer, who delighted in the young girl's precocious intelligence.

Emmy wasn't sure who Jacob resembled in disposition,

except that his temper fits sometimes reminded her of Isaac's brother, Winfield. Jacob was direct and always ran ahead. He needed to be watched and pulled back. More than once Isaac had to correct him and apologize for his son's interruptions into adult conversations. But she also mused that at least on one occasion, the person with whom Isaac had been speaking turned to Jacob and thanked him for his passionate observation. Jacob would become a fine young man someday if he survived. And someday, soon she expected, a delivery of books and a good slate board would arrive in Bellingham, and she could start teaching her children what they must learn if they were to prosper in this new land.

That week she received a letter directed to her from the Bellingham military commander, Captain Pickett, who inquired whether she could provide fresh beef for his forty-man garrison. He announced he would visit that week and, if she was amenable, wanted to inspect the cattle before consummating the order. He also wished to introduce himself and pay his respects. The order would be smaller by a third than the one they had consummated last year with the Port Townsend fort commander, who had ordered four hundred pounds of prime beef each week. She had always been surprised that the small garrison in Port Townsend could consume so much meat. But as she reread the letter, she suddenly realized he had been receiving his fort's allotment from the commander at Port Townsend, who was reselling it, likely at a significant markup, with some of the proceeds going into his own pocket. Captain Pickett had either discovered the little scam or unwittingly found the supplier, but in either case was trying to reduce his cost. By his florid language, she realized he was an educated man, and from his looped and gentle script, she could tell he was a sensitive one. He chose sad, ornate phrases. One sentence she reread several times in his official communication was, "I beg your indulgence, madam, lest I create an importune imposition on loyal hardworking settlers like yourselves, most certainly beset by the arduous work and sometimes desperate difficulties of surviving in this hostile land." He signed the letter, "Your most obedient servant, Captain George E. Pickett, Commandant, United States Army."

Thus bemused, she wrote back to him that she would be most pleased to sell him the beef and, without revealing that she surmised he was being swindled by the officer in Port Townsend, offered a price five cents less per pound than what she was delivering to the cheat. She and Isaac could afford the few dollars a week this was likely to cost them, if, as she suspected, Port Townsend subsequently cut back its order. And it made her smile at the propriety of such mischief.

CHAPTER SEVEN

◇◇◇◇◇◇◇◇◇◇◇◇◇◇◇◇◇◇◇◇◇◇◇◇◇◇◇

PICKETT

He had heard she was comely, a looker, by the description of one of the grain merchants with whom his supply sergeant was bartering. The merchant, a dour, unctuous, potbellied man with a pock-marked face poorly covered by a gray-yellow stubble, also noted that Emmy Evers ran her husband's business with a tightness that surprised anyone who casually might be taken in by her soft countenance. In his experience, the merchant said, if one tried to push past her civil and gentle demeanor, one found something quite durable, a "spirited filly" not easily swept aside by casual assumptions. Most men in the region believed she was the perfect complement to her mate, Isaac

Evers, a hardworking and honest dreamer who, until he had brought her to Whidbey, had little to show for his ambitions. After she married Ol' Isaac, the merchant said, things began to fall in their right place, and the entire Whidbey area started to prosper.

George Pickett was intrigued by this banter, and as he listened to it, he thought about what a good mate would bring to the unique loneliness he felt here, so different from what he had experienced in the parched Southwest, where he had buried his first wife. The perpetual gray skies of this area, the inescapable drizzle during the winter months, overwhelmed the little bit of disciplined fortitude he had at his personal command. He dreaded the oncoming winter and the gnawing boredom that drove everyone in the garrison to fits of mischief and frequent daylong drinking bouts with contraband whiskey obtained from local mill workers who helped load ships in the harbor. The last year had been particularly bleak, and he reprimanded himself for the example he set for his men. He had remorse for the punishment some of them endured because he believed, with some certainty, that he had contributed to their transgressions. He had built a home away from the post so he could find privacy and indulge himself without betraying the trust he was expected to build, but the whiskey did not cure the boredom. Now, with cold winds sweeping in from the Bellingham bay into the meager community, the locals were shuttering up the windows and themselves inside, bracing for another bitter winter. He kept himself busy, mostly by writing lengthy reports to Harney about local hostiles and the likelihood of their renewing attacks on settler communities.

Despite this, and over the next few months, curiosity

turned to an obsessed daydream, and he found his thoughts tugged to an image of Emmy Evers, constructed from what he heard from the merchant. Did she resemble Morning Mist or Sally, his first wife? Was her reputed steely constitution discernible from a distance? How deep was the soft shell that supposedly lay on the surface?

He decided to make an excursion south. Accompanied by his sergeant and armed appropriately for the hostile environs, he rode fifty miles along the coast, encountering both black bear and a small group of young, aggressive Lummis. The bear turned and ran away at the sight of the mounted twosome, but Pickett had to draw his saber and then finally fire a warning shot to get the natives to clear off. Remembering a bad experience with the Apache in Texas, when a similar encounter had been followed by a nighttime attack that had nearly been disastrous, he and his sergeant traveled ten miles beyond the site of the confrontation to provide safe distance between themselves and the Lummi youth. He would have given himself even greater berth if he were in the Southwest or the Lummi were mounted, but these northwestern natives were likely more curious than truly dangerous, he reasoned. Further south, in a natural safe harbor, he secured western waterway passage on a small logging boat to bypass the deep and treacherous channel they called Deception Pass that separated Whidbey from the mainland. One day later, they landed on the flat, sloped western landing on Whidbey that Isaac and Emmy Evers had created for their flourishing business.

Pickett didn't know what he was looking for on this trip, wondered whether Emmy would be demur and slight like his first and second wives, or hardened like most of the white women whom he had encountered in the Northwest. How did a reputed Northwest beauty compare to the women he had met over the years: the refined, wealthy ones in Virginia; the more adventuresome in Illinois and Ohio; and the aggressive, worldly wise women in New York? He tried putting that thought away and justified his trip with the notion of official and responsible discharge of business duty for the United States Army.

CHAPTER EIGHT

◇◇◇◇◇◇◇◇◇◇◇◇◇◇◇◇◇◇◇◇◇

EMMY AND PICKETT

She was surprised when Pickett arrived, as it turned out by coincidence, the very next day after she had sent off a response to his letter. When her neighbor's son, Stephan Crockett, arrived at her door announcing the landing of the two soldiers, Emmy ran upstairs, quickly washed off the morning labor's perspiration, pulled her hair into a tighter braided bun, and furtively glanced at her outline in the bedroom's vanity mirror. As she did so, she wondered at her motivations, deciding that such attention to personal detail was really in the best interest of her employing a disarming presence for negotiating an enduring contract with a reliable client. As she drove her buckboard to meet Captain Pickett, she determined to take measure of him against his ornate script. "Captain Pickett, this is quite a surprise. I received your letter last week and just yesterday sent a response to your query. I expect you and my offer passed each other out in the straits. I expect you will be pleased with our proposal."

He was dressed carefully, with obvious attention to detail, and she noted that he spoke with a soft and gentle cadence, less florid than his written word, but with a refined, precise selection of words nevertheless. "Madam," he said, with a doffed-hat bow, "I am most pleased to hear that, and I humbly beg your pardon for not waiting to receive a response. This was the most convenient time for me to go on this excursion. The weather will get inhospitably mean in a short time."

Hearing this gently voiced excuse, Emmy wondered if he also spoke this way to the men he commanded and watched the quiet exchanges between the captain and his sergeant, who seemed to respect his officer's orders. Pickett carried himself with a dignified solemnity that was unassuming at the same time. Emmy read a sadness that lay beneath his ornately designed ensemble. In contrast to the enlisted man, who looked as if he had slept for a fortnight in his dirty clothing, Pickett's uniform was proper, clean, and tailored with attention to detail, from his boots to the nonmilitary-issue cape that covered his shoulders. The difference told her that Pickett gave an almost dandylike attention to his own appearance but obviously was less concerned how the men he commanded represented him or his office. When she extended her hand to receive his, she felt hard yet small and carefully manicured fingers. His nails were clean and trimmed. She inhaled discreetly to sense whether Pickett used any cologne but could discern none.

Ordering the sergeant to drive the buckboard, he accompanied her back to the house on his beautiful gray mare, and it was apparent to her that he understood how to cut a dashing figure by his canter and carry. Indeed, as they proceeded up the incline from the beach and onto the homestead, he kept slightly ahead to her right in a privileged, very visible position, so he could not be ignored. He dismounted and quickly moved to the buckboard to help her down, and then, as the sergeant hiyawed the horses off to the barn in the back, waited before advancing further, almost shyly, until she had mounted the steps and beckoned him into the house. "Come along, Captain."

Sarah and Jacob, ever observant, were waiting on the porch stoop and watched Pickett enter after their mother. Following after him into the small, modest parlor, they stood expectantly until he noticed their presence, at which point Sarah stepped forward and asked to take his coat and cap. Pickett obliged and, seeing wide-eyed Jacob, winked at him, then unbuckled his field saber and handed it over to the boy. Jacob, duly impressed with this privilege, hefted the sword, three-quarters his own height, with a solemnity that made Pickett smile. The children quickly returned from their task, hovering, until Emmy motioned for them to go upstairs to their rooms. "Sarah, Jacob. Captain Pickett and your mother have some important business." She turned to Pickett with an apologetic smile.

As Sarah was about to turn away, Jacob stepped forward. "Do you ever fight the Indians, Captain? My father has. In the war east of the mountains. He's a colonel in the volunteers." Pickett knew about Isaac's participation in the fight against Kamiakin. All the military in the region had been grateful for volunteerism after the Elliott Bay attack, but the eager participation of untrained militia had caused its share of problems as well. After a similar attack on Bellingham a few months later, Pickett repeatedly had to intervene to rescue innocent natives from lynching by angry settlers. There were decent citizens and ones who simply made a mess, he thought to himself, and wondered into which category Isaac Evers fit. He squatted before Jacob, bringing his eyes level with the boy's, then glanced up at Emmy and Sarah. "Well, I heard that your father is a brave man, son. We try to avoid picking fights with the aborigines. I just try to keep order up in the north end of the sound."

Emmy gave Sarah a look, and with that Sarah took Jacob's hand and pulled him away. "That's enough, little brother." She turned and watched Pickett carefully as she guided her brother up the staircase.

Pickett stood until his hostess sat down in the small parlor's one soft-cushioned chair and then, after she motioned for him to be seated, placed himself opposite her on the divan, discreetly observing her motions and mannerisms. It was evident to him that she was with child, although early enough in her condition that her posture and gait were not yet tentative.

Emmy had finely cut lines and a smoothly curved back; sturdy but not overly broad shoulders; and strong, well-proportioned hands with long fingers, similar to the velvet- and lace-covered ones on the beauties he remembered from the cotillion ball celebrations in Virginia. He thought of his two wives. Sally, his first wife, born of a wealthy family and well bred, had had smaller hands than Morning Mist, but both women had had a brown hardness to their touch, developed from the toil necessary to get along in their harsh environs. Emmy Evers had the same firmness and calluses as the other women, but somehow she had preserved the gentility of motion from her well-born origin. Her face was finely featured with high cheekbones and bright, fiercely honest brown eyes that were fixed on his own in a way that discomfited him. Some women's eyes, he reflected, betrayed an angry self-pity and others a naïveté that made for contempt or tempted seduction. There was none of this in Emmy's deep brown eyes. Rather, he found them hard to observe because of what her eyes pulled up to his own surface, overwhelming him in an instant. He knew from the moment he met her that she would never let him get away with a lie.

"So, Captain Pickett, it is apparent from the soft cadence of your speech that you are a Southerner but not from the Deep South. I would guess the beautiful state of Virginia. Am I correct?" Seeing a flash of appreciative affirmation in his eyes and sensing in him the melancholia she had witnessed in others during this fall season of quick-darkening skies that followed on mellow Octobers, she nodded over to the parlor window and the slate-colored seascape below. "What does a Southern gentleman think of this sad green and gray?"

He followed her wistful glance and nodded. "Astute, madam," he smiled. "I would say that to one who rode for a few but, at the same time, too many years in the Southwest and on the baked Mexican deserts, the color green has always provided a welcome contrast for me. The perpetual gray skies of the winters here, however, make one almost forget the definition of verdant and what a full palette of colors can do for one's disposition." After a pause, he continued, "I miss my home very much at times, particularly during this change of seasons."

"I understand, sir. I understand."

That commiseration established a bond between them, and for a few moments, neither spoke. Their eyes moved again to the window. Then, for a short while, they exchanged a simple yet formal banter, with short forays into each other's perspective on a variety of subjects. They discussed each other's vision of what constituted propriety, God's purposes, and, as well, the destiny of their young country. Because of his mannerisms, more than by the words he chose on the topic of the political debate raging back East, she was not surprised when Pickett professed a deep disdain for slavery. She had found that, unlike other soldiers she had met, he worried for the welfare of the aboriginal inhabitants of the region. She heard him use the word "unwitting" repeatedly in his description of the unfortunate peoples' response to their rapidly changing living conditions. He was particularly vehement about his condemnation of how the Brits behaved in Vancouver, which he believed was greedy, despicable, and deceptive. She sensed that he held back criticism of his federal government, as likely he must.

"My husband, Isaac, believes the same as you do, Captain. While he is as eager as many to see our nation's boundaries expand, he believes we are part of a grand plan that must ultimately also include a fair outcome for all its creatures, whatever the original station in which they have been placed. That said, we have had difficult challenges, and he believes it is our burden to change all of that for the better, perhaps through faith and hard work. Perhaps through miracles."

As she said this, she thought about how Isaac's brutal encounters in eastern Washington had profoundly changed him from a young man with a cornucopia of enthusiastic, albeit undisciplined, applications of energy into a pensive, sober, and phlegmatic adult who increasingly found it difficult to finish the various projects he had started. It no longer amused her to manage him as she often admitted to herself ultimately had become her responsibility. Isaac, over the past year, had developed a fear of death, she realized, that now outweighed his sense of opportunity. In the early years of their marriage, she simply had listened to his list of ambitious projects and added an ordered, practical prioritization to them so that a good number of them actually were completed. But Isaac was stalled now. He seldom spoke of enterprise or the future.

Pickett responded, "As I believe I conveyed to your son, Jacob, my hopes are to keep confrontations minimized between all the inhabitants of this region. Although conduct as a warrior has been my calling, my experience has taught me that peace is always better, madam. And perversely, perhaps, it seems that assuring peace sometimes requires a stern, if reserved, intervention." Emmy considered this and understood that Pickett, at least by the words he carefully chose, had armed himself for those necessities and that, as a disciplined soldier, he likely had found a comfortable balance between self-preservation and duty. She wondered if poor Isaac, with all that he had seen, had it in him to fight in the same manner anymore. She wondered whether martial training amplified the appetite or, alternatively, resigned a man to the cruelties of armed conflict. In Pickett, she sensed the latter.

After a long pause, glancing again outside at a brooding sky, Emmy suggested to Pickett that they inspect the cattle as a prelude to a formal proposal on price. Then, because of the impropriety of offering him lodging in her home while Isaac was away, she told him about the plain but comfortable rooms that Ben Crockett generously provided for a modest fee to wayfarers. She then invited Pickett and his sergeant to have a meal with her and her children after the inspection of the Evers cattle. Pickett immediately accepted her kind offer of hospitality, and Emmy proved that her skills as a cook were as formidable as were her abilities as the manager of the family business.

That evening, during a dessert of apples crisped with cinnamon and caramelized sugar, she negotiated an arrangement: twenty-five cents per on-the-hoof pound, by which their farm would supply the Bellingham outpost with all its beef in the future. The captain seemed surprised that she offered him terms that were much more favorable than what he was paying to the supplier in Port Townsend, not realizing that the intermediary he used usually purchased the same Evers beef. Emmy knew, however, and again smiled to herself at the justice of this new arrangement. They shook hands on the deal, and Emmy realized, by that gentle clasp, that she had won his trust in similar manner to how she had won over every other man with whom she had business dealings. At the same time, she felt sad that he was so naïve and earnest a person that he could be so easily swindled by his military peers. He was likely a very brave and noble man but one with many gaps in his character that needed a complement to make him whole. That gave her pause and reconsideration, seeing that Pickett, like so many lonely men in this rough land, might need the help of angels after all.

CHAPTER NINE

∞∞∞∞∞∞∞∞∞∞∞∞∞∞∞∞∞∞

ISAAC

saac arrived home two mornings after Pickett had departed, ten days sooner than Emmy expected. He had beached his canoe on the northeastern shore far from the docks he had built further to the south and left the contents with the Negro who lived near the landing. Emmy saw that he was exhausted and pale, and, after he rounded the area by horseback, alerting the neighbors that trouble was in the waters again, Emmy helped him lie down. He slept for ten hours, barely moving during his respite. Winfield Evers, Tom Iserson, and the Crocketts shared guard that week, and Emmy took her turn. She knew how to shoot and did it as well as any man. The fifteen Whidbey families in five different parts of the island had worked out a simple plan so that, should a raiding party attack any one of the local cluster of cabins, warning shots would be fired and bells would be rung. The homes on Emmy and Isaac's plateau were close enough that a relay of shots would send the alarm quickly to all settlers who would be in harm's way. During the daylight, the children shared the duty of watching the water for signs of longboats.

Three weeks into the vigil, as the fall light started to fade more quickly on the broad fertile plain, Ben Crockett spied six longboats in the middle of the strait. They were heading north. He was certain he saw captives in each boat. In the preceding decade, before the smallpox had devastated the Northerners' ranks, the sight of six boats heading northward would have provided little comfort to white settlers and local tribes. But the straits had been quiet for some time now, and it was widely assumed that the presence of increased patrolling by British gunboats was acting as a sufficient deterrent. Besides, no reports from any neighbors had come in the recent weeks of any large groups of marauders.

Eight days later, Isaac took a small contingent of volunteers back across the sound to bury the Negro settlers. It was a depressing and grim journey, but Isaac reasoned it was the only decent thing to do, commenting to the few who protested that he hoped someone would do the same for him and his family if, God forbid, they ever were taken in the same way. Not far away from the site of the slayings, they found Sam's body. From the looks of his remains, he had fallen off an embankment, likely in the fog the morning he fled, breaking his neck, dying with swift mercy. Over the large grave they had scraped in the clearing behind the cabins, Isaac prayed for forgiveness from the Lord who had spared him but had taken these sad, frightened lambs. He regretted his curses against Sam. He put himself in Sam's situation on that horrible day, tried thinking in the same way as Sam must have thought. The fellow had never been malicious or lazy, and Isaac forgave him for his cowardice. Remembering his own terrible fear on that day, Isaac wondered whether God had heard the curses he uttered against the poor man, wondered whether God had answered those curses at the same time as He was granting him his own deliverance, wondered about God's strange way of showing mercy to him in that exchange, and told himself that his selfishness had to have had some purpose that he might not ever understand but that it was the will of Providence after all.

CHAPTER TEN

◇◇◇◇◇◇◇◇◇◇◇◇◇◇◇◇◇

ANAH

A half day before Ben Crockett had seen the longboats on the strait, two other Northerner boats,
commanded by Little Raven, split off to find
water and look for more to plunder. Anah led his six longboats, carrying fourteen captives, back north to the mouth of
the Campbell River. There he quickly sold the captives, all
young healthy women, to a trapper who served as an intermediary to a prostitution slaver. The trapper, Rene Marte, and
his companion, a huge, one-eyed Negro known as Cull, had
developed a number of similar business arrangements, including smuggling stolen contraband goods to the Tlingit and
Haida. Their prearranged contract allowed Anah to obtain

powder and winter supplies as well as the alcohol he would use to barter and stoke the rising anger of numerous tribal allies he hoped to recruit. He understood the power of alcohol and guarded it as carefully as a weapon, distributing it just before an assault. But he also always carried a small flask for himself into his initial parlays because that seemed to make things easier.

In Port Gamble, near a new sawmill enterprise that had imported forty Irish men and women to work it, Little Raven's raiders found an encampment of local natives, mostly Salish and Chimakum, who had converged on the small community. The Indian groups had come in gradually over the summer to see the mill, many out of curiosity, some for trading, and others for handouts. By August, over four hundred surrounded the mill, and the mill foreman had sent repeated requests to the forts at Port Townsend, Bellingham, and as far south as Olympia to see if some soldiers could be dispatched to disperse the encampment and avoid what the foreman perceived as an inevitable calamity. The coastal Salish, rich in some parts of the sound and numerous in diverse small bands throughout the Olympic peninsula, were being recruited by the powerful tyee known as Leschi and by other tribes to join in another attack on the Elliott Bay community and the white settlements further south, but thus far, the Salish had resisted. Still, incursions by settlers throughout the region were disturbing to the Salish because of the audacity of the whites and the arrogant contempt they all seemed to display at every official encounter. Leschi, in particular, was angry about a land and reservation treaty that had been consummated at Medicine Creek a few years earlier, which, he protested, he had never signed. To further aggravate the hostilities, Stevens, the territorial governor, had declared a war of extermination the previous year against the regional aboriginal tribes, thereby giving justification to both sides for senseless violence. As the white settlers increased in numbers, the disputes also increased, resulting in numerous deaths, reported and unseen. A few Jesuit and Obenite missionaries had established a presence and had converted a good number of the clans in the preceding fifteen years, but most of the Salish had resisted that too. Thus, they hadn't been exposed to the Christian concepts that likely prevented much of the conflict in other areas where the missionaries had built churches.

When Little Raven's raiding party found the encampment, it was already in a state of agitation, with arguments erupting between families over a variety of issues and old grudges as well as a few new ones, including the presence of the mill that many argued would soon attract more white settlers. That was fine for some, who anticipated the advantages of trade. But others argued that their freedom would be taken from them, as had happened to those living in the eastern part of the sound and in Vancouver. The whites were experts at that, they knew. The arguments were loud and hot.

Little Raven, despite an infirmity that year from a stroke that had left him with a clumsy left arm, still had his keen sense of strategy and immediately perceived opportunity in the making. Although the Northerners were likely not known by these Salish, he ordered the Haida and Skidegate in the longboats to remove their face paint, don clothing stolen from various raids against the settlers, and leave their canoes hidden in an attempt to conceal their identities as they moved through the Salish encampment. They settled into a secluded area on the long beach near a stream to rest and quietly observe. Because so many clans and tribes were present, tribal languages and dialects being spoken in the area were diverse, and thus many resorted to the Chinook trade jargon to communicate with one another. Observing this as an advantage, Little Raven, adorned with telltale double labrets on his lower lip and prominently tattooed, kept himself covered. He forbade his warriors to speak in their native Makan and had the least conspicuous of his Haida warriors be the spokesperson, conversing exclusively in Chinook when any interaction was necessary.

Thus, the Northerners' presence in the camp went unnoticed for several days. On the fifth day, however, a Makah woman, slaved to a Salish tyee, passed on the outskirts of the Northerners' encampment to retrieve fresh water. There she encountered a young Haida man bathing in the stream. At first, she was aroused by the warrior's well-proportioned, naked physique and, while observing from a thicket upstream, found herself flushing and faint. But after a few minutes, the young warrior turned to the front, and she recognized the significance of his tattoos, having, as a little girl, witnessed a terrifying raid by Haida against her Tatoosh clan. He was a killer. Each one of the tattoos told a story, and the way he bathed himself, watching with narcissistic pride as the water fell over his young, muscular body, instantly reminded her of a vicious experience imposed by similar arrogant men, likely from his clan, who had left her family decimated and enslaved. She hurried back to her own encampment and passed this information to the tyee of her small group, TsasiTa Na, also known as Trader Johnny. Johnny, well known to white settlers in the area, was a shrewd and enterprising man and, always looking for profit, decided to keep news of the Northerners from the other Salish. Instead, he sold it to the mill foreman. When the already frightened foreman heard the news, without waiting for full details, he immediately sent off a native messenger with a hastily scribbled letter to Port Townsend, where it so happened the steamer gunboat *Massachusetts* was docked, provisioning itself for a redeployment the next week to San Francisco. Arriving two days later, the message was misinterpreted by the commandant of the naval ship, who ordered an immediate departure to rescue the mill from an imminent attack by several hundred Northerner Indians.

By the time the *Massachusetts* arrived the next day, the encampment was in turmoil over other issues. That morning, several shots had been fired in anger by Salish men who had squabbled during a bone-dice throw, and two men were wounded. The mill workers, hovering nervously in their houses, heard angry shouts and yelling. Thoroughly terrified now, the mill foreman ordered all the employees to crowd into a blockhouse he had constructed for defensive purposes. When the *Massachusetts* finally steamed into the Port Gamble bay at three o'clock in the afternoon, the foreman signaled from the blockhouse that the camp was now under siege and had been fired upon.

The captain of the gunboat decided that the best way to break up the attack was to fire warning shots into the encampment woods nearby. Two fell short, killing several men, women, and children. The Salish natives fled in several directions, while the Haida, seeing their opportunity evaporate, gathered their equipment and ran up the beach to where they had hidden their canoes, hastily pushing themselves into the high, late afternoon surf. Because theirs was the only activity on the northernmost beach, it was easily observed from the *Massachusetts*. The commandant of the steamer, Captain Henry S. Melton, finally seeing an opportunity to destroy Northerner longboats within firing range, turned his starboard guns on the two canoes. He ordered canister and grapeshot rather than shells, anticipating that the scattered discharge would provide better hits than shells from the eighteen-pounders. Both of the fleeing cedar longboats were riddled badly in the cannonade but moved out of range of the *Massachusetts*, which by then had turned its attention back to the Indians on shore.

When the mess was complete, thirty-eight Salish and Chimakum on shore had been killed or wounded by the fusillades. In the canoes, Little Raven was wounded in his back and belly by canister shrapnel and suffered a slow, agonizing trip back north. By the time they reached the Campbell River, he was dead, along with six other Skidegate and Haida. And on the day of the Port Gamble massacre, Anah dreamed of his sisters again. This time they were blowing into the nostrils of Little Raven telling him to come back to the house because it was cold outside. But Little Raven refused to get up at their beckoning.

It was pouring down in a warm fall rain when the canoes arrived in their rendezvous place. Anah saw the drained, white body of Little Raven and, overcome by his angry grief, tore away his shirt, then ran into the woods and stayed there, naked, for several days. In lulls between cloudbursts, the Haida, preparing a makeshift funeral ceremony for Little Raven and the other warriors, could hear Anah in the distance, howling in a way that none had ever heard before. When he finally returned, he was covered with dried blood and the stigmata of self-flagellation and mutilation, fresh knife cuts along his legs and arms. He had pierced himself with branches through his ribs and chest. And he had a look on his face that never left him thereafter, a terrifying black mask of a stare, signaling to all an absence of any hope of mercy. When he returned to lead the ceremonies, he vowed in front of the other lead men that he would have the head of a big white tyee to act as a footstool for Little Raven in the next life.

CHAPTER ELEVEN

✕✕✕✕✕✕✕✕✕✕✕✕✕✕✕✕

ISAAC

News of the Port Gamble conflict reached Whidbey the next week with descriptions of destruction of Northerner canoes and warriors. The commandant of the *Massachusetts* reported a great victory and predicted that the bloody beating would finally end Northerner aggression, so demoralized were the survivors of the cannonade. Official reports to General Harney stated that the Indians around the mill, "mostly Northerners, had been given ample and repeated opportunity to disburse but had refused to do so," forcing Captain Melton to open fire. The captain did not mention that longboats had escaped and minimized the number of casualties that the natives had suffered. The ship's marines had placed several of the wounded Salish, unable to flee into the forests, into irons, and the captain made a big show of transporting them out of the region and depositing them on a small island southeast of Victoria, presumably to perish. Without interpreters, he never realized that none of his captives were Northerners.

When the Whidbey settlers heard the initial reports about the events in Port Gamble, most assumed the raiding would stop, at least for the rest of the year, because the weather would soon preclude canoe travel on most of the sound. Their reassurance was based further on common knowledge that the Northerners had always avoided direct confrontation with better-armed foes, and the presence of a fast steamer gunboat like the *Massachusetts*, independent of the wind, exceeded the ability of the raiders to move quickly in any weather. If the gunboat patrolled the sound, as they had assumed it must henceforth, the Indians would desist. They did not know that the *Massachusetts* was bound for San Francisco in one week. They also did not fully appreciate how important revenge for wrongdoing was to the Haida and all other tribes.

Isaac returned from his burial detail to a settlement much relaxed from the week before. The Whidbey families had seen no other longboats. The regional *Colonist* newspaper had reported that a large contingent of northern marauders had been clapped in irons and taken away. Hearing the stories related to the Port Gamble battle, Isaac smiled at heaven, which had surely sent an answer to his repeated requests to General Harney, Governor Stevens, and the numerous legislative contacts he had in Olympia.

Isaac had good reason for his requests. For the past two

years, since the attack by several tribes on the Elliott Bay community, most of the naval patrolling had been done with small, slow-sailing gunships that concentrated on the south sound, where numerous tribes still were considered hostile. The thirty-four-gun *Decatur* war sloop that had saved the Elliott Bay settlement during the attack had long since departed the Northwest waters. The United States Navy did not have enough ships deployed on its long West Coast to patrol all the waters it now owned, and General Harney, without ever creating any formal agreement, had decided he would leave the major responsibility for containing the most hostile of the aborigine tribes to the British navy, which by contrast had established a formidable presence in Victoria. Yet the Brits seldom ventured into southern Puget Sound ports. The sporadic violence that every settler anticipated as a risk of pioneering could not be predicted, and thus it was almost impossible to interdict. And so, the Port Gamble events and the reassurances that had come from them did, indeed, seem like a godsend. But Providence had not established a real balance.

Four weeks later, in late October, immediately after a three-day deluge with high winds that toppled men and trees alike, two Indian visitors, an elderly man and woman, landed on Isaac and Emmy's western-facing beach, just south of the small community on the plateau. Dressed in pioneer garb, each wearing long pants and red calico long-sleeved shirts, they bore no visible markings on their faces or hands. Speaking in Chinook, they found a local Salish native, Jim Thomas, who occasionally worked for Emmy, and queried him about where they might find the local physician, Dr. Joseph Edwards.

Edwards, trained and apprenticed in Philadelphia, had settled on Whidbey three years before and had established a widespread reputation for compassionate homeopathic care. He delivered his potions and repaired broken bones with enough success that some even sought his opinion on other, nonmedical matters, traveling from as far as Elliott Bay and Bellingham on occasion for his consultation. He, like Isaac, had developed a good amount of influence on legislative processes in Olympia, and both men had more than once been mentioned as possible gubernatorial candidates to displace Stevens, the mercurial politician who had commissioned war in eastern Washington against several tribes and had infuriated even friendly native populations with his inflammatory rhetoric.

But Edwards was not at home that day, having departed in the morning for the south of the island to sit up with a young woman confined in the last stages of a first and very difficult pregnancy. Normally, Edwards would have relegated the delivery to a competent island woman, Jenny Searing, who had a good amount of midwife and wet nurse experience. But this baby was malpositioned in its mother's belly and just wasn't descending as it should, so Edwards was going to try to rotate it for a head-first presentation to minimize the risk of delivering a breechling or stillborn infant.

Jim Thomas explained to the couple that he had seen the doctor depart, carrying medical equipment with him on his Morgan filly. They seemed disappointed with his answer, and when he asked what they needed, the couple responded with a question about whether any other big tyees like Edwards lived in the area. Pointing toward Isaac and Emmy's home, Thomas told them that a very important tyee lived in the house on the bluff, then went about his fishnet mending. The couple departed back down the beach.

The wind from the western strait always blows easterly in the early evening on the prairie plateau. On that evening, it kicked up earlier than usual and then settled down by seven. Isaac was in the woodshed when the Indian couple appeared at his picket fence. His big old Labrador, Rowdy, began barking loudly, bringing Emmy to the door. Because of the dog, the couple did not advance farther than the fence and asked Emmy if they could borrow a hammer and some nails so they could repair their canoe down on the beach. They seemed surprised when Isaac came around the house to see who was talking. The man, sturdily built with a hard and pockmarked face, turned his attention to Isaac. Both visitors looked at Isaac carefully from foot to head, as if measuring him, Emmy noticed. The woman, weather-beaten and almost toothless, repeated the request, adding that she wanted to buy some sugar or molasses and coffee. Emmy sensed a nervous, stilted manner in their speech and heard a dry sticking hesitancy in the man's enunciation of the Chinook. Isaac paused, glancing over at Emmy, then told the couple they did not have a hammer or nails nor did they have any food supplies to spare. So the couple turned and left quietly without a word. Rowdy finally stopped barking when they were out of sight down the pathway to the beach. Isaac thought no more about it. Natives and wayfarers occasionally stopped, and none had ever created problems. Emmy thought the couple was odd but turned her attention to the dinner she was preparing.

A few hours later, the guests arrived, including Tom Iserson, his wife, Rebah, Major Robert Campbell, and his wife,

Thomasina. The company ate two full helpings of Emmy's roast beef; shucked and cob corn; a fine spiced, late summer squash compote; warm bread with freshly churned butter; and the clove-spiked pear pies from a recipe Emmy had brought with her from her grandmother in Boston. The major introduced some decent English port imported through San Francisco, and all partook, offering a pagan libation to the change of seasons, followed by a brief prayer of thanks to God for sparing Isaac from harm on his recent journey. They talked about many things, including the dispute with the Brits that was heating up over the ownership of San Juan Island to the north, and the perennial congressional strife over the Negro slavery question. Campbell and his wife, originally from Alabama, expressed strong sentiment for allowing new states to determine their own rulings on that matter. Iserson, always the wiggling Whig turned Republican as Rebah liked to refer to him, believed new states should be accepted into the union only if they agreed to be free from the evil curse of slavery. Despite entrenched positions on the matter, the discussion was civil and quiet, with the two sides holding onto their positions and each agreeing on the other's right to disagree. By half past ten, the Campbells begged their leave, noting they had early morning chores, including completing repairs on a roof that had started to leak in the past week. The Isersons lived too far away to trek up island in the dark, so they excused themselves to the guest bedroom in the back.

In bed that night, watching Emmy pull her brush through her

hair, Isaac thought about all the things he had witnessed during the past several weeks and how rapidly events changed in this world, teeter-tottering, it seemed, from pain to fortune, and how much that had benefited him and his family. If he could persist, surviving the challenges that Providence had in store, he would keep moving upward, he knew, being righteous in the presence of the Lord on his judgment day. He just had to endure the sufferings because God would balance it all. That was the plan and the pathway. And it was working. Only a short while ago, he had been a penniless gold miner looking for opportunity in uncharted territory. Then, using the surveying skills he had learned in Ohio, he'd mapped out the inland lake east of Elliott Bay and later, on Whidbey, had acquired the best piece of land in the Puget Sound region. Certainly he'd had his pain, losing his first wife, Rebecca, to a tumor that had grown in her breast and had just eaten her away in less than a year. He couldn't watch her in those last few weeks—the seepage and smell of rot, seeing her suffering, weeping out of her mind until she just didn't recognize him or anyone else, blind and wasted.

But he had found Emmy not long after and moved her up from Olympia where she had been stranded by the carelessness of her late husband, who had allowed himself to get whipsawed by a falling tree near the big mill he had constructed in Tumwater. Isaac, visiting Olympia as a north Puget Sound representative, had seen her at the funeral and, from that first moment, knew he had to have her. For a very young woman, she carried herself with repose and dignity, and she was absolutely stately in black. From a discreet inquiry, he learned that she was a well-born Boston Irish, who had rounded the Horn with her new husband, an ambitious, wealthy, and extravagant dreamer twenty-five years her senior. The gossip was that they had shown little affection for each other, and some thought she was lonely out here in the cold, wet green, despite the wealth his venture had brought. She would head home after this, taking her infant child back to a wealthy civilization.

So Isaac did what he had learned worked for him when he needed something badly. He took a gamble, sending a card to her the following week, asking to speak with her. Emmy came to the door at the cedar-clad home by the mill she now had to dispose of, expecting another solicitation for purchase of its fallow equipment. Instead, Isaac, hat in hand, offered her a large bouquet of white roses and told her, "My name is Isaac. I live up north on Whidbey Island where I have staked out the prettiest, most fertile land in this entire Northwest. I am a strong, prosperous man. Please. Please do not return to Boston. Stay here. With me." That was the hardest and most insane thing he had ever done in his life. But it was the best thing he had ever done as well, because she took the roses.

About two o'clock in the morning, Isaac awakened from a dream that left him in a cold sweat. He was running down a long beach after a woman. It was Emmy. She had turned and looked at him in horror. "Wait, Emmy. Can't you see it's me? Wait!" Then she got that look only she could have. Fierce. Resolute. That was all he could remember as the scene faded away. It was then that he heard Rowdy barking, behind the late October night wind that had started up again. Sometimes Rowdy would holler at raccoons or deer wandering up from the beach. But this time it was persistent and anxious in a way that frightened Isaac. He reached over for his shotgun and remembered he had lent it to Tom Iserson for his watch last week and Tom had brought it back with a broken hammer. So, stuffing his nightshirt into his pants, he picked up a large walking stick and felt for the bedroom door. Emmy was awake then, asking after him. "Isaac?"

"Rowdy is making a lot of noise," he said, descending the stairs to the front door. He looked out the window onto the porch. "Visitors" was all he said. He lit a lantern, picked up a knife from the kitchen table, then opened the door and stepped out onto the porch.

CHAPTER TWELVE

◇◇◇◇◇◇◇◇◇◇◇◇◇◇◇◇◇

ANAH

Jim Thomas was almost finished mending his fishnet when the old Indian man and woman came down the path from Isaac's house. They walked fast and passed him without words or thanks, pushed their small cedar canoe into the light surf, and turned it about, heading north. They were out of sight within a few minutes, and Jim thought nothing more of it as he gathered up his thread and netting. Only a few days were left to get into the water before the cold November swells would be too big to fight.

Three miles from the beach, out of sight of the small settlement, the Indian couple turned shoreward and found a quiet cove, not dissimilar from the one Isaac had settled. There they met up with a medium-sized war canoe, ten warriors, and Anah. The old man and woman beached the canoe, stripped off the long pants and shirts, and reclaimed their jerkins and furs. Anah and the warriors intently watched the old man—Klixuatan, the clan's shaman—who seemed in no hurry to impart news. Then the old woman, his remaining wife, started to chant, and Klixuatan began a song and did a small five-step dance. They were singing to the raven god for a new special strength, and then all the warriors knew they had found the big tyee. A few minutes later the sun dipped below the Olympic Mountains, casting a red hue onto the water. Anah knew the omen was good. Blood on the water.

Over the next five hours, they chanted quietly to a clan song led by Klixuatan. "Moon bird running quick, bringing back the day and all our children. Water giving moon a second life."

When the half-moon showed itself, Anah and four of the warriors stripped naked and painted themselves with bear grease and red ochre from head to their ankles. They pulled the ornaments from their labrets, whet their knives on beach stones, rechecked their powder, and then pushed off southward in the larger canoe. The cold would keep them alert.

They did not sing any of their clan songs en route; instead, each warrior had his own private song that he hummed to himself, synchronized by Klixuatan, who tapped the side of the canoe with each dip of his oar. Anah had moved into a trance during this part of the journey, and while he paddled, the ugly events of the past year rushed past him. Forging the coalition with other tribes had proven more difficult than he had anticipated, partly because so many of them also had been devastated by the smallpox scourge, but also because, under his leadership, his own clan's predatory actions over the past ten years had diminished the number of aboriginal tribes willing to deal with him. In the grand wake of events, with incoming settlers, aggressive actions of the British and U.S. governments, inventions and addicting conveniences that had to be assimilated, and new diseases that had to be endured, aboriginal groups were suffering and desperately reeling throughout the entire Northwest. Anah also felt alone ashe never had when he was younger. Over the previous twelve months, with the loss of so many companions and then Little Raven, his past and the map it provided had been torn away from him. With the deaths of so many of his children, it was as if his horizon had disintegrated as well. He thought of this as he beat his syncopated rhythm against the side of the canoe. He knew that each warrior in the canoe carried the same burden. He would regain all of the hope for future bounty that rightfully belonged to them and snatch happiness back from the white intruders who had stolen it so viciously. He would cleanse away the shame.

Anah had never been afraid of Death because it was always around him from the time he was a small child. Instead, he played with it as if it were a curious friend that hid behind every living thing and showed itself when he called it forth, when Anah cut into the flesh hard and deep enough. Over the years, he had killed enough men, women, and children to know the measure well. And, understanding his special friendship with Death made him an exception to all other men with a privilege that had to be revered and honored, he had attempted to visit Death several times on his own, off away from where there was movement or noise, deep in the forest, away from the interference of other spirits. Knowing he could only really speak with Death if he offered himself, he beckoned to it with his own blood and starvation. It always ended with him alone again, the conversation incomplete. But each time he understood more. On a few traumatic occasions, he had been impulsively driven there, as when he had received Little Raven's wrecked body and when he beheld the charred bodies of his children in the smoking remains of his burned-out village. In his grief, he had run as fast as he could into the forest hoping to catch Death, knowing that in so doing he might look one more time at the spirits of his loved ones. But he was never fast enough.

As a complement to his companionship with Death, in a lesson he learned on many journeys with Little Raven, he always had the comfort of others like him who understood. The ferocity of their every action was a language that endured and resonated universally with all creatures. All who followed him understood this. By their clan's actions, they defined and marked out their close proximity to Death and their status as its favorite companion. His actions in a fight, and those of the few who were privileged to learn from him, were direct, immediate, and instinctively centered on an opponent's most vulnerable weakness. He knew his foes would invariably expose it by their protective actions. And then Anah would immediately counter with vicious decisiveness. Anyone who tarried to think, aim, or react was simply swept away. The deliberating actions of the whites were cumbersome compared to his own instinctive tactics, so none of his lumbering opponents ever survived. Such was the ability of Anah, who lived with Death as an ally.

They reached Isaac and Emmy's beach as the moon reached its zenith, darting in and out from a cobweb of blue-black clouds. They pulled the canoe far up the beach because the tide was coming in and left Klixuatan to guard it and protect their passage away from this tyee's magic. Each man draped himself with an otter skin nooksack and, carrying their rifles, clubs, and knives, moved up the beach to the pathway that Klixuatan had indicated led the way to Isaac's home. It took ten minutes to traverse the pathway onto the plateau. Isaac's home was first, prominently perched looking over the entire plain from a short, cresting, north-facing hillock. In the moonlight, intermittently revealing the harvest stubble of the manicured land, several cabins were visible in the distance, but no lantern light or fires.

As they drew closer, a dog began to bark from behind a white picket fence. Closer still, and then a light came on inside the house, and a tall, powerfully built man came out onto the porch. Anah knew it was the tyee he had come to kill.

CHAPTER THIRTEEN

ISAAC AND ANAH

When they saw each other at that moment, eyes locked in the pale moonlight, each man knew the world had stopped around them to watch a death dance. No sound, no movement, just the focus of equals carried quietly over several heartbeats. Anah knew in that instant, because of an aura of vibrant life surrounding his opponent and this homestead, that he was now closer to Death than he ever had been before. It would come rushing forward eagerly, he knew, and take one or both of them.

◇◇◇◇◇◇◇

Isaac knew he was staring into the face of his own personal exterminating angel, and from that realization, he thought of protecting his family. Before he could call out a warning, the tall, naked savage moved first, leaping over the picket fence, clubbing Rowdy aside, then bounding up the steps to the long porch, aiming with his ball club for a finishing blow to Isaac's left temple. Isaac, watching his attacker's fierce eyes, saw the blow coming and ducked away. From a stooped position, he thrust his heavy walking stick's butt with an upward blow into the man's sternum, knocking him off balance. As the attacker staggered back, Isaac followed with a roundhouse swipe with his knife that caught the man's left pectoral chest, cutting deeply into the muscle. But not deeply enough, Isaac knew. He saw that the pain from the laceration seemed to energize his assailant, and, spinning away, Isaac saw him reclaim his balance and move forward onto the deck. He swung again, but lower now, at Isaac's neck. Isaac ducked again, but this time the attacker's heavy ball club, razor-sharp spikes jutting from three sides, struck him with a bone-crushing thud on his left temple. The blow carried him over the rail onto the yard below. He hit the wet sod, wrenching his neck and left shoulder, but quickly pulled himself back up, still holding the heavy walking stick. As he righted himself, preparing for the man's next blow, two younger warriors simultaneously discharged their muskets at him. One musket ball struck Isaac in the chest, fracturing his clavicle, and the second blew off the thumb of his left hand. Isaac was thrown back but kept his feet. Holding his bloodied hand to his punctured head, he stumbled toward the ocean-facing side of the house.

As soon as the bullets hit, despite a numbing confusion and a searing pain that pushed deeply into the back of his head and down into his neck, Isaac knew he would not survive this fight. That one thought defined the rest of his existence. In his confusion, he had lost his sense of direction but somehow stumbled to the side of the house where there was no door. As the big aborigine and the four others rushed at him, Isaac struggled to hold up the heavy walking stick to ward them off and detain them a few moments longer. But he knew he had done his duty. His family might escape from the other side of the house.

Anah was upon the white tyee and this time used his knife in a jabbing movement to Isaac's neck, cutting directly and deeply into the wound made by the musket shot. The knife severed first the jugular vein and then the carotid artery. Isaac collapsed and fell forward, his hand still holding his head, eyes rolling up at his heaven. Anah took a handful of Isaac's long, blond hair and pulled his head back, then cut his throat in one swift motion, at the same time motioning to his companions to break into the house. As they turned to the house, Anah cut again deeply into Isaac's neck and, in five quick, practiced motions, severed his head from his neck. Isaac's heart, still beating rapidly, emptied itself in less than thirty seconds. Anah had seen this before, although not with such a big tyee. In his triumph, he lifted Isaac's head up and turned its face toward him. In the cold moonlight, he saw Isaac's head open its eyes briefly and close them slowly with a look that startled Anah so much that he gasped and dropped it onto the ground, knowing he had been cursed in a way that would haunt him forever.

CHAPTER FOURTEEN

<><><><><><><><><><><><><><><><><>

EMMY

Moments after finally crawling under the covers that night, Emmy fell into a deep sleep. She had been sick all day, starting in the morning with dry heaves. She knew it was the pregnancy souring her stomach. The bleeding had stopped a few days before, and Doctor Edwards suggested she might just keep this one, if only she would rest and hold food and water down. The nausea made it difficult for her to prepare food for dinner because she couldn't stand even the smallest tastes to sample her work and couldn't concentrate on the recipes. After dinner, she had not participated much in the lively conversation and had excused herself to clean up the kitchen. She hated the political discussions and, in particular, had a difficult time tolerating the pontifications of Tom Iserson, who never would let anyone forget he had studied at a prestigious seminary in the Midwest for two years before moving west to prospect for gold and, although he wasn't ordained by any church, had converted aborigines to his personal interpretation of Christian redemption.

Emmy had put the children to bed shortly after dinner and, because the participants in the parlor were very loud during their impassioned conversation, she was not surprised, when she checked on Jacob and Sarah, that both were awake. They had been listening to the adults in the parlor debate about whether Governor Stevens's call for extermination of the aboriginal natives was evil and impractical or just plain stupid and provocative. Sarah, grasping the significance of the political instability of a hotheaded leader, had asked her mother whether Isaac would be nominated for governor as she had heard some folks suggest. Emmy had just smiled and told her daughter that a nomination was the least of her stepfather's concerns.

By the time she had returned to the parlor, Major Campbell had opened up a bottle of English port and poured six small glasses. Despite her nausea, Emmy accepted the offer and sipped it politely as the conversation turned from politics to news about the gold strike on the Fraser River near Vancouver, and finally to gossip about the large Catholic family that had moved onto the southern part of the island. Shortly after the clock struck ten, the Campbells begged their leave, and only a few minutes later, Rebah and Tom announced they would retire as well. It was just as well because entertaining the Isersons without the genteel cushion of the Campbells would be a chore, and she was already exhausted.

When Rowdy started barking a few hours later, Emmy was in the deepest part of her sleep, settled in a place that was comfortable and familiar. But it wasn't in the Northwest. She was visiting her family in Boston, and her father and sisters were at the parlor table waiting for her to come in from the garden with Isaac, Sarah, and Jacob. She had arrived first, and Kate, her oldest sister, had that impatient, bothered expression on her face that she had always used to keep the younger siblings in a state of perceived inadequacy. Kate was looking past her at the kitchen door, and Emmy turned to look for the entrance of her little family. But she could only hear the children, bickering over some silly thing. She waited for Isaac to correct the children and then formally present himself to her family. What was taking him so long, and why was he not attending to the children?

As the dog's barking grew more frantic and insistent, she incorporated that nuisance into her unfinished dream. She saw that Rowdy had cornered a raccoon in the big Italian plum tree that grew outside her parents' brownstone window. He was jumping up at the treed angry creature and snapping and grabbing at the big plum, stripping pieces of bark from its trunk, as if that would somehow dislodge the hissing coon from its perch. She heard Isaac then, and she hoped he would shoo the pesky little bandit away quickly so she could reassure her family that she was married to a reliable man.

But Isaac made so much noise fumbling around in the dark that she suddenly felt the hard bed and remembered she was not in Boston at all. She felt anger at Isaac for his inconsiderate clumsiness, waking her from the first good sleep she had had in a week. She was about to murmur a chastisement, but as she turned to him, she realized his movements conveyed anxiety. It was enough to rouse her. Still hoping to return to the colors of the dream, she pulled herself out of bed and pulled a blanket around herself, following him to the stairs. As she stepped into the hallway, she stubbed her right great toe badly on the doorstop, peeling her toenail back. That wakened her fully, anger spilling out with a curse at Isaac who had already reached the bottom of the staircase and was fumbling with the lantern. He did not respond to her and seemed to ignore her pain and anger. When she saw him pick up a kitchen knife, trepidation replaced the pain. "Isaac?" she called down to him. The expression on his face as he looked up briefly told her he was determined but frightened. As he opened the door and stepped out onto the porch, she immediately thought of Jacob and Sarah and rushed to their room. There was a window facing the front yard, and from there, she could see what was happening.

Jacob was already awake and looking outside when she entered. As she walked in, he gasped; she heard Rowdy yelp in pain, then silence. There was a loud jostling on the porch below. Jacob cried out, "Indians!" and Emmy was now fully functional. "Run! RUN!" she heard herself scream so loudly that Sarah awoke immediately and, without questions or protest, headed for the stairs. The cry awakened the Isersons, and Tom emerged from the bedroom downstairs naked, wearing only his socks, with Rebah following.

"RUN, children, run!" Emmy cried again. Iserson, hearing the fighting outside, ran to the back window and, his face contorted by his uncontrolled panic, pushed up the sash and jumped out, leaving his screaming wife and everyone else behind. The first gunshot shook the house.

Emmy heard horrible, vicious screams from the porch outside and knew Isaac was fighting for his life—and for theirs.

CHAPTER FIFTEEN

◇◇◇◇◇◇◇◇◇◇◇◇◇◇◇◇◇◇◇◇◇◇

JACOB

They all followed Iserson, who by this time had leaped the backyard fence and disappeared into the brambles up the hill and into the woods. Jacob watched Rebah Iserson running after her husband, screaming for him to wait for her. The moon cut through the clouds for just a few moments, giving his mother her bearings as she ushered him and his sister through the blackberry thorns in a different direction, toward the small road that led up to the Crocketts' home a mile away. Jacob could hear the marauders now in the house, crashing through the kitchen and over-turning furniture, but he kept running as those sounds faded away, running, knowing that just behind him on that same path Death would be pursuing him silently and relentlessly. He could not see his mother or sister now it was so dark, and Rebah kept bawling for Tom someplace off to his left by the big woods. He heard his mother holler out in the darkness, "Run, kids. Get to the Crocketts. Run!" but he couldn't tell where her voice was coming from. He was old enough to reach that destination without directions, if he could find the pathway beyond the blackberries that crossed the cattle pasture. And then he stumbled onto the path. As he struggled to stand back up, he heard careful footsteps behind him. Mother? The last thing he remembered about that night was the strong hands that covered his mouth.

CHAPTER SIXTEEN

◇◇◇◇◇◇◇◇◇◇◇◇◇◇◇◇◇◇◇◇◇◇◇◇

EMMY

After she called out, Emmy lingered a bit, telling herself that if there were pursuers, she would jump in to protect her children. As she reached the pasture, she saw no one on the path but heard grunting noises that made her remember the young stud bull that was supposed to be penned up in the barn. Big, stupid animal that protected that field, studding and crapping. Always took three, sometimes four, men to get it back into its pen. Worth the trouble, she had always told herself, because of the extra poundage his offspring carried. Tonight it was an ironic bit of fear to add to the terror.

The field was uneven, and each step tore at her wretched toe as she continued running toward what she hoped was the Crocketts' home. Where were the kids? Where were the kids? Then she heard Sarah screaming out up ahead. They must have reached the Crocketts. Emmy ran past several squawking geese and knew she was there too, past the small brown fence and up the stairs. Sarah was pounding frantically on the big oak door. When Sarah heard the footsteps behind her, she gasped but then released her held breath when she saw it was her mother. They pounded on the door together, louder now, hollering out for Crockett to awaken. Emmy turned, looking for Jacob, Rebah, and Tom. Heard Ben's voice from inside, "Hold on! Who the hell is it?" When he opened the door, he had a big knife in his hand, and Missy Crockett stood behind him with a twenty-gauge shotgun pointed at them.

"My God, it's Emmy and Sarah!" He pulled them into the house, peering past them into the darkness.

Sarah cried out, "Northerners! Father was fighting them, and we had to run."

"My God!" Crockett blurted out, looking down at Emmy. "Em, you're wounded!"

Emmy thought he was talking about her foot and then looked down to where he was staring. Her nightgown was covered with blood from the waist down and was dripping all over the rough-hewn floor. Missy looked at Emmy's white face, handed the shotgun to Crockett, and said, "Ain't a wound, Ben."

CHAPTER SEVENTEEN

◇◇◇◇◇◇◇◇◇◇◇◇◇◇◇◇◇◇◇◇◇◇

EMMY

The bell rang louder now. It had a name finally; "Nagger," she wanted to call it. Emmy had slept hard, and it took hours it seemed to wake fully again. When she came about, the room was still, but she could hear voices quietly talking. Moving in the bed, she caught her wretched toe again, and the dull pain brought her back to herself. She felt a bandage covering it, dulling its sting. She wondered if she were dead because the morning nausea that had bothered her for the past several weeks was gone, now replaced with a weakness that went all the way down into her bones, pushing her right through to the floorboards. The whispers continued, heated now it seemed, but too muffled to understand. Was it Northerners? Did they just come to pay respects and negotiate a deal for the cattle? Where was Isaac? This mattress was softer than hers, and she knew from the embroidered, quilted cover that she had to be in Missy Crockett's home, maybe her bed even. She was embarrassed to not be in her own bed and felt like an intruder, like someone who, just to get a moment's rest, might have slipped through the window in the night. She needed to get out of there. Where was Isaac, and why weren't the children up running about and fussing as they always did? She was wearing a different, clean nightgown, but she was wet hot. She threw the quilt off and pulled at the gown. The bell clanged outside again, longer now. Nagger. She called out to the voices, which stopped abruptly.

She sensed someone outside the door. After a few moments, Missy Crockett pushed it open and entered with Joseph Edwards. Both wore concerned and sad expressions that cut right to her chest. Missy immediately sat down at the bedside, took Emmy's hand, and smoothed her damp hair. She was holding back tears, Emmy could tell. Joseph Edwards had a gruff, clumsy way of saying things for a doctor, but she always knew he meant well. He knelt down at eye level with Emmy and reached over to touch the top of her hand hesitantly. "Emmy, it is so good to see you awake. I was beginning to worry that the combination of the ether and sedatives I used might have been too much." Then he touched her forehead. Turning to Missy, he said, "She's burning up. Get some rubbing alcohol and water and wet her down."

He paused, seeing Emmy struggling to understand. "Dear, you lost the baby. And now you've got an infection that's going to put you to the worst test you've ever had."

What was he saying? She tried to form words but her mind seemed full of cotton, then slowly, around the edges, the terror returned. Everything was coming at her at once and she wasn't even sure where she was. The baby? As she stammered out "the baby?" Edwards interrupted her. "You have to preserve your strength and rest. Please drink this down," he said, lifting a cup of apple juice to her mouth.

Emmy then remembered she had been pregnant, and the misery pounded her down harder than when she had lost the first baby two years ago. Somewhere from another room she heard a man's baritone laugh. Isaac?

Edwards paused, watching her closely, "Isaac and Jacob are fine. Now rest." But she hadn't asked Edwards about Jacob, she thought, as the drift from the laudanum overcame her and she was in a field by herself, counting and losing count.

CHAPTER EIGHTEEN

◇◇◇◇◇◇◇◇◇◇◇◇◇◇◇◇◇◇◇◇

JOSEPH EDWARDS

A practitioner familiar enough with the benefits of ether surgery, Dr. Joseph Edwards had put Emmy under when her miscarriage was inevitable and she needed help clearing out the clots that followed the small stillborn fetus. With the bleeding stopped, he was now worried about the morbid fever that followed bloody miscarriages like this. Sometimes the woman survived, but so much depended on her residual strength. Frail ones passed in a swift night, shaking and melting away in front of the bereaved. But Emmy could beat this; he knew because of the temper of her mettle.

He had been called on the morning of the awful attack, after Ben Crockett, Winfield Evers, and a few men from the east side of the island had ventured out together to be certain the marauders had cleared. When they went to the Evers' homestead, they had found Isaac's headless remains. Edwards had gone to the Evers home before attending to Emmy because it was on the way to Ben Crockett's house. But just for a few minutes, because he hated violent death scenes. The men had brought the broken carcass into the ransacked house to keep the crows away. He had seen decapitations before. Felt it was such a robbery of a body's dignity. On Elliott Bay where Edwards had first started practicing, before Evers convinced him to move to Whidbey, there had been several decapitations after a twenty-five-dollar reward had been posted for the head of the Indian who had raped and killed one of the Elliott Bay settlers. Eighteen heads, all likely taken as retribution for miscellaneous grudges, had been brought in before the settlers realized the bounty had been a mistake. He had seen some of the heads returned to the families of the deceased. The headless bodies always seemed so much smaller and foolish looking. This desecration was no different than others he had seen— thumb missing, a big hole blown out of Isaac's back from a heavy slug, likely a .54 caliber. The body wouldn't have survived that wound anyway, so the missing head seemed irrelevant, except that it wasn't. When the burial took place on a body rotted away from a cancer or simply dwindled into a frail carcass, he always imagined the full person in good health no matter what. But this was so hard to put to rest.

By the time he got to the Crocketts' twenty minutes later, Emmy had collapsed, and Ben had carried her unconscious upstairs. She was bleeding heavily and had already passed the fetus, which Missy Crockett had wrapped in a new linen next to a votive candle, lit for its tiny soul to find its way to purgatory. Edwards inspected the fetus and saw that the small placenta had not pulled away intact from the uterus, which meant that Emmy would continue bleeding and die unless he could evacuate the fragments along with any large clots left. He took a bottle of opiate from his bag and told Missy to mix a half bottle into a pitcher of water and then to arouse Emmy enough so that she drank a full tumbler. After Emmy ingested the mixture, he soaked a handkerchief wrapped around a large cotton ball with ether and held it over her mouth and nose. She didn't struggle much. When she was limp, he began searching for the remainder of the placenta.

He lied to her about her husband and son because she needed to sleep through this infection. The searchers hadn't found Jacob, and now they were walking through the underbrush in the west evergreen woods near the Evers house to see if he turned up or was dead. A day after the attack, Tom Iserson had emerged from the woods and came walking up to the Crocketts, naked except for his right stocking, babbling biblical verses and profane curses. It took a full two days to find his wife, Rebah, cowering under a fallen tree, crazed, bawling her eyes out, broken down. The men had to talk to her for an hour before she would come out. Jacob was nowhere to be found. Edwards, watching Emmy struggle with a fever that most likely would consume her, decided it would be best to order the burial of what remained of Isaac Evers. He would keep Emmy heavily sedated and deal out the terrible news when she was strong enough to receive it. His lie would not matter if she passed on, and he would be spared the pain of telling her the truth.

Edwards officiated over Isaac's burial the next day, Sunday, October 22nd. Islanders had come from Whidbey's four corners, arriving with gifts and condolences for Sarah and Emmy. By the time the ceremony started shortly before noon, a near freezing rain blew its bitter bite across the fertile homestead that Isaac and Emmy had so successfully developed. Winfield and Ben brought the cedar plank casket up from the Evers home, then all the men who had been standing by waiting moved over to help lift it off the carriage and lower it into the drenched grave. Corrine Evers, Isaac's lame sister, and Missy Crockett placed a large wreath of rosemary onto the casket as it passed by. After the men pulled the ropes out from the grave, as the cold rain started pounding the earth and water pooled around the edges of the coffin, they picked up shovels and covered it. When the last shovelful had been placed, Edwards stepped forward to speak: "We all knew Colonel Isaac Joseph Evers. He was a handsome, hardworking, visionary man. He helped all of us settle in this rough land. He and his wife, Emmy, created a homestead that is the envy of everyone here. It is a tragedy that his great effort and love have ended in this way. God has a purpose. Dear Lord Jesus and God Almighty, watch over Isaac in his journey and take care of his family, in your wisdom and mercy. Amen."

That was all. No one else spoke. The cold rain was fitting to the horror of the past several days, and the neighbors and friends had already said to each other what needed to be said. Those who knew Edwards expected no more words. Sarah left with Corrine across the plateau to stay with Isaac's brother and his wife.

After the mourners had departed in their carriages, Jim Thomas stepped out of the cedar pine thicket north of the gravesite. He carried a small bundle to Isaac Evers's grave and pulled back the loosely packed dirt near the grave's marker. He unwrapped the woven bundle and placed its contents into the hole. It was a head, roughly carved out of cedar, its eyes painted in with blackberry juice. As he covered it up, he sang a little song in Salish: "Go into the dark place with these eyes open. With these eyes open."

CHAPTER NINETEEN

<><><><><><><><><><><><><><><><><><><>

EMMY

Was it Isaac? She heard him first before she saw him, and as she got closer, walking through the madrona saplings through a fading light, he made a raspy sound that reminded her of his sighs when he had expressed his most desperate doubts about his life. Each step toward him made him seem to move farther and faster away, and when she pushed aside a low-hanging deodar branch, she was in a dark clearing about fifty feet at its widest. She saw his back moving out and away, deeper into the woods. He was weeping, she could hear. As she crossed the pine needle floor to follow, she heard a cry from a long way off to her right: "Mama!"

Was that Jacob? When she turned to locate the sound, she saw a black-red shadow emerging from the clearing not far behind her, close enough that she could hear it panting and smell its fetid exhalation. She stopped, hoping it would pass by her while she held herself motionless. But it stopped too, and she could see it was watching her from its cover. Then the cry again. Her eyes moved in the direction of the sound, and she forgot for a moment that she was being stalked. When she looked again, the shadow was gone. Had it swept by? Where did Isaac go? Why was he crying and running away? Where was Jacob? Sarah, go get your brother, she struggled to say, but the words wouldn't come out.

She woke for a moment and found herself in the still of a dark room. It wasn't hers, and then she remembered she was in Missy Crockett's home. She was dripping wet; her nightgown was soaked. She pushed the light cover off and lay there exhausted, looking up at the pinewood ceiling, its rough textures becoming clearer as her eyes accommodated to the early morning light. It felt like a big coffin. Why was she here? Where was her family? She tried to get up from the bed, pushing herself up by the elbows, but the room faded away again.

She was on the shore looking out at a gray chop, peering into the northern horizon, up past the huge snowcapped mountain range to the west. What was she looking at? She knew it was out there, whatever it was that had brought her down here, facing the chill and cut. She knew she had been watching for it for a long time, and yet, she understood that she had just gotten down to the shore a few moments ago. She saw it coming toward her place, getting bigger against the dull whitecaps, and as cold as she was already from the icy angry gusts, a chill drove deeper straight through to her backbone. She stepped back across the beach, unable to pull her gaze away, and then stumbled back onto a barnacle-encrusted rock, cutting the heels of both her hands.

It landed on the shore a few feet away from her and began chopping with its large beak, a massive black crow that floated halfway into the water. It hovered over her for a moment, dripping salt water and saliva, and then swept past her up the track to her home. She pushed herself up, tried to cry out: Run, kids, run! but nothing came forth. Ran up the path but could not get her footing and kept falling backward, backward again and again, back onto the stones below. Where was Isaac? She clawed her way up the pathway, one agonizing pull after another, and when she got to the top, she saw that her home was gone. It had never been there. She wiped the sand off the cuts with one quick swipe and ran back down to the beach. The specter had receded and was moving away along the coast, back north. It was carrying something on its back and in its beak, and she knew they belonged to her.

On the third day after Isaac's burial, Emmy's fever broke. She slept heavily for two more days, intermittently waking, alternating between delirium and mute silence. Missy Crockett, Corrine Evers, and an Indian woman named Princess Susan attended to her, bathing her and changing her linen. Missy and Corrine brought Sarah in with them as often as possible. She was old enough to see someone struggling with a horrible illness, and the women had agreed that Sarah's constitution was much like her mother's, so she would only grow stronger with witnessing something as difficult as this, whether Emmy lived or died.

Edwards instructed Missy to gradually start reducing the laudanum. He had seen many women die during postpartum fevers and, believing that Emmy had a chance, had kept the women working the poultices, mustard plasters, and cooling baths, watching and logging every change in her movement, color, and excretions. She had lost enough blood in the miscarriage that Edwards did not believe additional bloodletting was wise or necessary, and he had been pleased that the discharges from her private areas had never changed to the sulfurous smell that usually preceded a terminal change. So he let her rest.

The next day Emmy woke for a few minutes while being bathed and brightened when Sarah came into her view.

She was on the plain overlooking the pastures and farmland. She wore the breeches she used when working the cattle in the pens below. A cooling breeze swept up her legs and pushed orange-red maple and yellow aspen leaves swirling about her knees. Across the plain and into the sunset, a tall man walked toward the western beach landing and disappeared over the cliff. She was now there at the embankment's edge overlooking the shore where she had previously seen the raven specter. The man was Isaac. But it wasn't him. And then he was gone. She looked northward again.

Emmy awoke the next day, and after eating a few bites of her first solid food since the night of the attack, she asked Missy to take her outside. Doctor Edwards and Ben carried her to the porch and set her on a chair prepared with blankets and a comforter. It was a warm late-autumn afternoon. She could hear the cattle braying in the distance and saw a big eight-point buck walk down across the plain and back up into the woods that bordered her fields. Corrine and Missy fussed and talked about doing a press of cider from the apples. She saw Sarah crossing the pasture with Winfield. Edwards was watching her. He pulled her lower eyelids down, looked at the creases on her palm, felt her pulse, and stepped back, hesitating.

Emmy looked up at him and at Missy. He stepped forward: "Emmy, Isaac's gone. Jacob's been taken."

"I know," she said.

Three days later, Emmy was strong enough to walk about, and the next day she asked to be taken to the gravesite. Edwards and Crockett lifted her off the buckboard, and Missy accompanied her and Sarah halfway, then stepped back when Emmy waved her away. Emmy stood there for half an hour, holding Sarah tightly and peering south across the hillside resting place onto the magnificent gently rolling homestead below. She knew that Isaac had died protecting her and her children. All the suffering and success from hard work and vision, the discipline to fashion chance and opportunity into a measurable and sustainable fortune, the heritable hope for her family—all of it had been destroyed in one night by cruel acts she still did not understand. Who were these people? What was God saying to her by this event? Why did Isaac fight instead of run? Did he know he was going to die? Was it a sacrifice? And why hadn't she helped him? Why had she been so cross with him for awakening her and fumbling around in the dark? Why had she run and abandoned him?

Her thoughts circled back again to Jacob. Why hadn't she kept Jacob by her side? Where was he? Was he hurt? Did he know about his father's death? Did he know she and Sarah were alive? Was he hungry? Was he cold? Was there someone in that savage crowd who would care for him?

She wept. And for the first time since she had surmised from her dreams the dimensions of her personal tragedy, she felt a release that cleaned out a muddy confusion about what she could have done to protect her family. She looked west, out toward the strait, remembered the dreams about herself on the shore, then pulled Sarah closer.

It rained for five straight days and nights. One week later, word came from Port Townsend that a British provisions ship had sighted two longboats heading north near the Campbell River. They had veered course and closed on the ship. The crew braced for an assault, but the longboats kept out of range of the ship's small cannon and ran parallel to the ship's course. The captain reported that through his telescope he glassed ten men in each boat and a small white boy in the second canoe. In the first longboat, a tall warrior, left arm in a sling, stood facing them. In his right hand, he defiantly held up a severed head.

CHAPTER TWENTY

<><><><><><><><><><><><><><><><>

JACOB

The two longboats moved north, keeping close to the eastern shore of the sound. When they passed the first cluster of Lummi fishing houses south of Bellingham, they moved in closer, and Anah had his warriors push their way into the shallow harbor, which berthed a few lumber ships and small fishing ketches. Several Lummi canoes lined the shore beside racks of dried salmon and halibut. It was 6:00 a.m., and the water moved slowly with a mild outgoing tide. As soon as the Haida rowers got within hailing distance of the fishing village a mile away from the larger lumber vessels, they began chanting and beating their oars against the sides of their canoes. They fired two shots that rumbled across the still water, breaking the morning's peace. As curious Lummi natives and white settlers emerged half awake from their shacks, the Haida began hollering and jeering. Anah, in the lead boat, held up Isaac's bloodless head and screamed, "Tyee. Tyee." The longboats then paddled out of the harbor moving northward. They repeated this at every village they encountered along their trek toward the rendezvous point near the mouth of the Campbell River.

Jacob had fought his captors as soon as he regained consciousness on the first night and, despite being a small child, had doubled over two of the warriors with swift kicks to their groins. One of them, the younger of the two, pulled a knife, but the other, holding a bleeding wound to his chest, had waved off the younger and given orders to the others in the encampment. Thereafter, Jacob was kept bound and slept during the journey north, drugged with a mixture of alcohol and herbs by Klixuatan's wife. On the sixth night of the trek, he awoke to the woman's quiet, rough voice singing a song he did not understand. As his eyes became accustomed to the darkness in the smoky tent, he heard the patter of rain hitting the lean-to's sealskin covering and found himself next to another boy, a frail-looking towhead, possibly a year older than Jacob's five years. The boy, also bound at feet and wrists, was coughing and shivering. "I'm sooo cold," he said.

Jacob looked about but could not make out much. He could see the flicker and shadow of a fire outside the tent, and he could smell meat roasting. He was hungry. "Please help me.

I'm so cold," the boy beside him said again. Jacob didn't feel cold. He looked at the skins covering the boy and realized that he had more coverings on him than Jacob had himself and wondered how the boy could possibly be feeling cold. The boy started coughing again, and his teeth began chattering. Jacob wanted to say something but drifted off to sleep. When he awoke, it was starting to get light outside. The chanting had stopped. The boy next to him was breathing intermittently now with a wet, raspy gurgling choking with every inhalation. Finally, it quieted down and then stopped altogether. Jacob slept. When he woke up again, he was alone. Where had the boy gone?

He came awake again with a bitter taste in his mouth and realized he had been fed. It reminded him of berries and salmon, but it was rancid and stuck in the back of his throat. He felt like throwing up. Now he was in the back of the longboat, facing forward for the first time, and could feel the rain and wind kicking up as the men rowing the boat quietly pushed steadily ahead. Where were his mother and father? Where was he being taken? He looked at the markings on the inside of the canoe. They matched the tattoos he had seen covering the body of the old woman, now faded and sagging into an ugly indistinct story, that of beasts fighting and devouring each other, crows crowing, whales with big eyes and rounded teeth, animals with angry blank stares in the middle of a fierce battle.

The old woman, wrapped in several skins and a wool blanket, sat next to him. She stared forward, singing to herself in a simple and repetitive chant. It was the same hoary voice he had heard when he was sleeping in the tent next to the boy who was coughing. He dozed off again but awoke with a start as he heard hollering. The men were excited and talking loudly, pointing off to his left. He tried to sit up and saw several killer whale fins crest out of the water ten yards away. Some of the whales were small, while others were big enough to capsize the large canoes. But they just moved on. After a while, the men calmed down, and the silent paddling continued. It rained for what seemed like a terribly long time, and then it stopped. In another hour, the sun came out, and the clouds seemed to spread apart showing off the land to his right, and after another few hours, the boats moved into a small cove and beached. He slept in the boat.

The next morning, he awoke to shouting as utensils and camp supplies were being thrown into the longboat. The early sunlight had just spread over the cove, and he saw the warriors looking past him out at the harbor. Jacob turned and saw a small ship flying a British flag resting at the south end of the bay. They shoved off and moved to the right of the harbor, heading north. He saw puffs of smoke from the ship, heard deep popping sounds, and then saw large splashes approximately one hundred yards short of the lead boat. The men in the canoes started jeering. He saw a warrior in the lead boat climb to the front and hold up a long pole. On top of the pole was a head. "Boston Tyee. Boston Tyee. Boston Tyee!" they all started hollering. The ship spread its sails and made way, and for a short while, it seemed to be gaining on the rowers. But the wind failed, and the ship fell back and began to recede from view. Soon it disappeared around the bend of the coast. Jacob watched for signs of the ship but did not see it again.

Two days later, the longboats reached a rendezvous point

where Jacob saw nine other longboats beached along the shore. As they came closer, the men in the boat began to chant loudly, and the camp on the beach came alive. He heard them shout, "Tyee!" The old woman nudged Jacob, looking to the front of the long canoe, and he saw the warrior in the lead boat mount the trophy on the pole again. Jacob, groggy from the cold, the drugs, and hunger, saw it was his father's head. His gaze followed from the waxen head of his father down the pole and saw the man who held it up staring at him intently. Anah.

CHAPTER TWENTY-ONE

◇◇◇◇◇◇◇◇◇◇◇◇◇◇◇◇◇◇◇◇◇

SARAH

She looked in the mirror and, for the first time, saw a face that was older. In the past, she hadn't spent much time grooming or preening, so a mirror was simply a place to look for tidiness. But over the past four weeks, with the burial of her stepfather and helping her aunt and Missy care for her mother, it seemed that her self-awareness had diminished so much that when she saw her face again for a moment, it was really a stranger looking back at her. Something else was different too; she had two white hairs, one on each side of her head! How could that be? She was only ten. She fingered them along their entire length, feeling if they were different in other ways. She pulled them out.

It was a relief when her mother regained her strength and was able to move about. Emmy had recovered quickly. As much as her Aunt Cora and Missy Crockett fretted, Sarah knew her mother would recover because she had never let anyone or anything best her. Sarah could never imagine her mother dying. Emmy had too much living to do. In many ways, Sarah had always sensed that her stepfather was vulnerable and would go long before Emmy. When he had been away in eastern Washington, Sarah had prepared herself for hearing that he had died in some massacre or by drowning or from snakebite. He always put himself out a little too far and didn't look out for himself as much as she thought someone should. Long before he died, she had imagined herself at the graveside with the mourners, all saying sad praises for his departed soul. And she would cry and have to wait to see him again in heaven. She had practiced crying for that event, and it felt sad the first time and less so the second time she did it. She knew about death, of course. She had seen animals slaughtered, remembered when that farmhand was trampled, and had seen Jimmy Falcon's washed-out body pulled from the sound when he and his brother had capsized their boat two years ago while fishing too early in the season. She understood the grief that relatives showed, and that was why she had practiced doing the same for the time when her father would die—so she could do it right and with some dignity. And when it happened, when Cora told her that Isaac was dead and Jacob had been stolen and her mother might die too, she had taken it in and knew the practice had been useful. She hadn't expected Jacob to be hurt, and she knew her mother would survive, but she had practiced weeping for Isaac, so she got through it and all the people told her that she was a brave girl.

But she was just doing what she had practiced.

How would she find Jacob? Would they hurt him or slave him or turn him into a savage or feed him to wolves? What would he be like if she got him back? Would he be different? Would he have grown white hairs too?

CHAPTER TWENTY-TWO

◇◇◇◇◇◇◇◇◇◇◇◇◇◇◇◇◇◇◇◇◇

EMMY AND
PICKETT

Three days after she heard about the sighting of
the longboats near the Campbell River, Emmy
received an army change order requisition in beef
shipments. Beef was to be shipped to San Juan Island rather
than to Bellingham. From the transport agent, she learned
that Captain George Pickett was under orders to move most
of his command to San Juan to establish a fortification in
anticipation of a dispute with the British over control of the
region. She also learned that Pickett would stop for a fortnight in Port Townsend to complete filling his supplies and

await reinforcements from Oregon. She decided she had to act quickly before a distracting engagement between the Americans and the British ensued and she could not get assistance in retrieving Jacob. Accompanied by Sarah and Winfield Evers, Emmy booked a short passage to Port Townsend and requested a meeting with Pickett and the commanding officer of the fort.

Winter was early, and when Emmy and her party arrived, snow had already covered the pine and cedar forest around the fort. Pickett was surprised by Emmy's visit and made himself immediately available, meeting Emmy and Winfield in the temporary office he had been given for his stay. He had only heard about the attack on Whidbey the week before and had struggled with a letter to Emmy, uncertain over the proper response. He had written three versions, each proper but incomplete and empty of the feelings that confused him all the more in the face of this tragedy. When Emmy arrived, he was still debating whether to send the last version, which offered to visit her at some point in the future to express his condolences in person. Would she accept that offer?

Pickett looked at Winfield, a bantam redhead with a tense, angry posture, and immediately dismissed him as a weak, unworthy, and annoying distraction. But when he saw Emmy, he noticed that her mourning black reinforced the power of her eyes, and he felt immediately overwhelmed by her again. He tried to remember the terms of the arrangement he had made with her and recalled that it had been a hopeless negotiation for him from the start. He didn't remember a whit of it, so taken with her as he had been, and when he had inspected the Evers cattle with her, he had bumbled his way through the transaction, peeking at her in a way that made him feel like a schoolchild. So here she was again. And her earnest expression made him turn away, to hide the blushing he felt. When he regained his composure, he looked up and saw Winfield glaring impatiently at him.

"Captain Pickett, thank you for receiving us," Winfield said. "You know about what has happened to our family. We need your help. I want you to dispatch a contingent of soldiers, perhaps an expedition, to hunt down the brutal savages who kidnapped my nephew and killed my brother in the prime of his life, a man who contributed greatly to the safety and prosperity of so many in this region."

Pickett listened but did not respond. He knew his expression obviously conveyed annoyance at Winfield's request. As he listened, he watched Emmy. What would she need? What could he possibly do to help her?

Winfield, reading Pickett's resistant expression, went on, tears welling up in his eyes. "Surely the military has some leeway in matters like this. This was not a common infraction or a random act of violence. This was a vicious attack—and this was my brother. He was a heroic man, and society is in debt to him and his memory. This was cold-blooded murder. It was an insult to the order that you are here to preserve, Captain. They decapitated him! We had to bury him in that condition. We have heard they have been parading his head all up the coast for the past two weeks. And who knows what has become of my nephew. We have modest means and do not have the wherewithal to establish rescue and retribution. But you do."

Pickett calmly measured his response. "Mr. Evers, I am, of course, very sad about the tragic events that have befallen your family. I share your concern about the safety of our citizens. Unfortunately, I am under orders to quickly establish fortifications on San Juan and will be unable to provide any of our resources. Perhaps in the spring we can discuss this again."

Winfield persisted. "You do not understand, Captain. This act, if it is allowed to go unpunished, will be seen as weakness on our part to citizens and heathens alike. That will, in turn, certainly provoke additional violence. The military has a chance to do something heroic and greatly symbolic. Acting now will convey a stern message to all the aborigines and reassure all loyal whites."

Pickett simply shook his head and smiled. "You have my answer, Mr. Evers."

Winfield could not contain himself. He stood up, his fists balled before him. "Captain, were I but a single man without family obligations, I would venture forth myself and take on these heathens. I would bring them to justice. This is a sad disappointment, and I shall bring this matter directly to Governor Stevens for help, to overturn your decision here." He turned, pushed open the door, and walked out, slamming the door behind him and storming past Sarah who stood outside in the hallway, leaving Emmy and Pickett in the room.

Emmy looked at Pickett, who seemed to be chagrined, perhaps embarrassed for her as well as for himself. She maintained her composure, however. "Captain, Winfield is highly educated and likes to show that off, but he also has always been a tempestuous man who seldom thinks before he speaks, although that was better than most of the exchanges I have witnessed over the years." She forced a small smile, cracking past a stern sadness. She paused, then continued. "This is no small request, I understand. My son is missing, and we believe we still may have the opportunity for rescue. We have been informed that this event was likely the work of a well-known renegade band of Haida. They winter up north, on the mainland across the strait from the Queen Charlotte Islands. I am told there are neutral trading camps up there too, with the Bella Bella and Tsimshian. We could send emissaries offering a bounty. I have a small amount of gold I have gathered that would likely be more than enough to establish a fair trade for my son. If it were possible to retrieve the rest of Isaac's remains, his head, I would bring that back too so it could be put to rest . . . where it belongs. But Jacob—he is only five."

She saw that Pickett listened to her carefully measured but passionate request. He sighed deeply, and a sadness seemed to come over him that told Emmy the answer. He stood and moved over to Emmy before he spoke.

"Mrs. Evers—Emmy—I am so very sorry. There is no way that I can help you at this moment. We are told by reliable sources that the British plan to send several companies of marines to fortify their claim on San Juan Island over an incident that recently occurred. I have to get there first and hold that ground. I have no choice in this matter. I cannot spare a single man."

Emmy studied him for several moments and then stood. He was telling her the truth. "Thank you, Captain. I am disappointed, but I understand." After a pause, she said, "I shall book a passage and will go there myself then. Without the help of this government. As you know, I am quite capable, and I negotiate quite well." She saw his concern. "I am not afraid."

Emmy turned and left, noting that Pickett seemed stunned at the directness of her pronouncement. She found Sarah sitting outside the door, took her hand, and made her way to their quarters.

As she did so, she shuddered, and an intense anger swept over her. She knew the captain was duty bound and had accepted that before she had even asked for his improbable assistance. Still, she had had to make an attempt lest the dutiful, but insane, course she planned be criticized. She had rehearsed the request as well as the response upon being denied assistance. She would not play upon Pickett's emotions as she knew some might. She had wanted to say to him, "Jacob is my little boy," but she prevented herself from making that final wrenching appeal. She knew she would keep that phrase to herself and she would be repeating it over and over again privately as she had for the past several weeks. It would guide her and drive her. And now she had many things to do.

That evening Pickett couldn't sleep. He thought about Emmy making her way far northeast into the aborigine winter encampments and the grim likelihood of her finding nothing but suffering and disappointment at best and, at worst, savage and brutal treatment and a painful death. He had failed to extend anything that might bring her some hope or intervene to dissuade her from this madness.

He thought of himself making the same effort. Wondered if he would ever have the temerity to overcome the inertia of doing so, letting go of the security that even the rudimentary civilization of this region provided. Could he, would he, ever take on such an arduous task for anyone he loved? Of course he could, he thought. But in his entire life, he could not think of one instance in which he had done so—put himself in harm's way for someone he had loved. He had risked his life for glory, certainly, and for orders, but he had no recollection of tempestuous acts for the love of woman or child. Did that make him bad, practical, or just selfish? He wondered what it was about love that could compel someone to such actions. He had conceived a child, a boy, with Morning Mist. He was fond of the child but felt no pride or devotion to him. He wondered if that feeling would have been different had the boy not been a half-breed. Thought about whether he had ever understood or accepted the weakness of his feelings instead of containing them as dangerous out-of-control calamities waiting to uncoil themselves, snakes in a box with its latch broken. He had seen men withered and besotted in a drunken, shrunken state in the aftermath of what they called love. He had detested it when he let himself go like that, had fought and always defeated that weakness, and thus wondered whether he had ever really been truly in love in the way that seemed to drive so many. He had been in sadness, certainly. He recalled that he had been head over heels enraptured by Morning Mist and had wept when she had died. But was that what they called love? Or was it rather an infatuation followed by the profound loneliness that comes with deprivation and self-pity? Had he ever been so compelled by his feelings for her, or for his first wife, that he allowed himself to defy logic or counter reasonable orders? If being enraptured was the same as being in love, he did not know how far he could trust those wondrous, terrifying feelings—of letting go. He felt so much comfort in the presence of order, determined by a rational set of calculations, grounded in a mathematical precision that pushed aside emotion. He thought love was the antithesis of order and the settling peace that accompanied it.

But Emmy's determination drew him to think of her, and he could not put that out of his mind as he slept restlessly. What did she need? Did he, by oath of his station and office, have a responsibility to her as a citizen, one that superseded his responsibility to follow his orders? Did he, drawn as he was to her by his admiration for her qualities and equanimity, need to preserve her for his own peace of mind or, for that matter, some future opportunity? Did he, from his notions of chivalrous behavior, have a sacred duty to protect her as a vulnerable woman? Could he extend his best efforts so that she might not suffer in her insane quest? How could she, the very epitome of order and control, framed in a wondrous sturdy and symmetrical visage, risk herself so? By morning he still had not answered his many questions and self-doubts, but he took it upon himself to seek out Emmy with what he had concluded.

When he found her in the trading post that afternoon having a calm yet intense discussion with the provision merchant, he was again struck by her beauty. He waited for her to finish her bargaining and then stepped forward, doffing his hat and extending a flourished but gentle bow. "Madam Evers. May I speak with you a moment?"

Emmy turned to him and, with a glance, dismissed the storekeeper. She nodded to Pickett and stepped to the corner near the dry goods section, then turned back to face him, waiting.

"I know you will not be dissuaded, Emmy. I respect that. One part of me wants to defy my own orders and go there with you myself. But I cannot do such a thing. You know that. Another part of me wishes to extend a protecting wing over you. But I believe I know you would not accept that from me, or anyone. I have little to give to you other than a recommendation for a guide and this." He handed her an ornately carved and inlaid box. "Please take it with you. It has proven to be reliable."

Emmy opened the box. Inside was Pickett's pepperbox pistol, a Belgian-made six-barrel Mariette, and a note with a name on the envelope. She looked at Pickett and nodded. "Thank you, Captain. Best of luck to you also."

Pickett watched her leave and carried to bed with him that night the image of her fierce resolve pushing her forward into dark winds. He did not believe in prayer, but he would pray for her nonetheless.

✧✧✧✧✧✧✧✧✧✧✧✧✧✧

CHAPTER TWENTY-THREE

EMMY, SARAH, AND MARTE

In the port, Emmy booked a passage the next day on the *Pietrevos*, a Russian trading ship bound for Japan but scheduled to stop in Fort Simpson to drop off supplies and pick up whatever furs were still being harvested in the region. It was a large, clumsy vessel with ample room for extra passengers. Its captain, Vladimir Varienko, a swarthy, tub-bellied lout with a greedy, incisor-dominant, salivating smile that immediately made her feel unsafe and uncomfortable, was more than willing to accommodate her. She had purchased supplies and chests of trading goods to buy her way into the Tsimshian tribe's winter camp, which served as a neutral trading place used by all the neighboring tribes to exchange supplies. She also carried with her a small box of gold coins minted in Philadelphia, a diamond, and several semiprecious stones that would be part of the final exchange with the Northerners, should she be given the opportunity. Knowing that Winfield had angry, vengeful designs that likely would thwart any chance for a trade, she asked him to take Sarah back to Whidbey and plan on joining her in a few weeks. She reassured him she would find assistance from the Brits and meet him in Esquimalt with Jacob. Sarah protested vigorously and pleaded with Emmy to allow her to accompany her on the recovery of her brother, but Emmy knew the real danger of this quest. She told Sarah that their best chance to find Jacob was if she went prepared to travel beyond Fort Simpson, quickly moving upriver for the encampment if necessary. Sarah did not seem convinced and sobbed angrily for a while, then suddenly quieted down and spoke no more of the matter.

The ship moved out on the next early morning tide and, despite a strong headwind and tumultuous high seas, reached Fort Simpson three days later, on the evening of January 4th. Confined to her cabin, Emmy had tried to write in a journal but mostly slept when she was not sick. She hated sailing, and this short trip brought back the horrid memories of sailing around the Horn, so terrible a journey that she vowed never to return to Boston unless she could go by land. She thought of Pickett and wondered how he would fare in the future, saw his confidence diminished in her presence, and wondered whether he was like that with all women. By his calm handling of the brief confrontation between him and Winfield, she knew that the killer in Pickett could dispatch most men easily. But she wondered about his deference to women, realized his chivalry was genuine, and that it made him exceptionally vulnerable. She thought of Isaac. As painful as it was to bring his memory forward, she forced herself to do so. He always had been so willful—predictably running down foolish paths so often but with a fervor that usually won him allies, outworking most and outwishing everyone else. In the last few years, she had hated seeing that part of him broken down, the stubbornness persisting so that it was read by others as a weak and brainless perpetuation of his vision. She knew he had never been a prudent man and that his proclivity to put himself directly in the path of danger, usually for the excuse of enterprise but more likely just because it justified itself, probably had caused his death as well as contributed to her miscarriage and Jacob's kidnapping. He had left without saying good-bye and without asking for her help. She was finishing his business again at great expense, and it made her angry.

It was snowing hard now, covering the decks with an inch of frozen blanket, and once the ship had been secured in the inner harbor, it settled quietly into its anchorage, sleeping finally after a long journey. Emmy looked out from her cabin window onto a moonlit scene that resembled a Christmas painting of a seaside village, much like the ones she had seen in an art exhibit as a child in Boston. She would be ferried ashore the next morning, and she fretted for the wait she had to endure. Perhaps Jacob had been sighted. Perhaps the British authorities had news or already had even intervened in some way. She had heard that such a thing had happened before, across the strait on the Queen Charlottes two years before, when a British surveying expedition had made an exchange with one of the Haida clans for two Vancouver children who had been snatched earlier in the year. Perhaps Jacob was in Fort Simpson already. She looked at the small town and said a prayer to St. Jude, whom she was told the Catholics considered the patron saint of the impossible.

Two hours later she was awakened by a loud knock at her door. It was the first mate. "Come. Captain has something belongs to you." Emmy followed the mate up to the snow-covered main deck and then aft to the captain's quarters. Varienko, dull-eyed—obviously awakened from a drunken sleep—wearing a filthy smock coat, and shoeless, was slouched against the doorway of his cabin, waiting for her. As she came closer, he leered at her, eyeing her up and down in a way that made her reach up and pull her robe tightly across her neck. Then he pushed open his door. Sarah, covered with soot, pale and anxious, was sitting next to his cabin stove, shivering. Varienko belched.

"Eet appear da lyetel gyurl want to companyou, Meezus Hyevers."

With a terse apology and an offer to reimburse him for the extra passenger, Emmy turned to take Sarah back to her cabin, and as she did so, she noticed Varienko followed both of them with a strange sly perusal. Emmy was furious. She pulled Sarah across the deck and down to her cabin in the aft hold. "How could you do something like this after I told you how dangerous this could be? How could you?" She stopped talking, poured water into the small basin on her bed, and proceeded to vigorously start scrubbing Sarah's face of the soot from the coal bin in which she had hidden. But if embarrassment and anger had overcome Emmy, her fury with Sarah's actions was short-lived. In her cabin an hour later, while grooming Sarah's hair from the knots and grime, she heard another knock at her door. It was Varienko. He held a bottle and two pewter goblets, and his britches and underpants were off, fully exposing him. He pushed his way into the room. "Meezus nyeets a dryenk with captain." Then he grabbed both Sarah's and Emmy's wrists and fell forward onto Emmy. In the screaming, angry struggle that ensued, Sarah wrested herself away. Without a pause, she quickly picked up the bottle he had dropped and struck him with it squarely across his right temple with such force that it broke into several pieces. He collapsed to the side of Emmy and did not get back up. Stunned, Emmy pushed herself up and looked at Varienko. Had Sarah killed him? When Varienko groaned half a minute later, she sighed in relief, then recovered her wits. She and Sarah dragged Varienko out to the deck, bolted their door, pulled out the pepperbox, and held each other closely all night, listening to the commotion outside an hour later as the crew discovered their inebriated, bloodied, and snow-covered captain on the deck.

The next morning, the first mate ferried them across the harbor and deposited them with their belongings on the wharf. He did not make eye contact with either of them during the entire passage and left them without a word. Emmy did not register a complaint, fearing retribution. The *Pietrevos*, with its cargo loaded hastily by a crew on double time, was gone by the evening's tide.

Emmy learned quickly that the only lodging available was at a small tavern-inn, the Red Pelican, on the west wall of the fort. She had sent word to the fort's commander to query assistance but was told that he and most of his staff were south in Victoria participating in an official reception for the territorial governor. She also learned that no hostages had been rescued or sighted in recent weeks.

The Red Pelican was a simple establishment, with rudimentary accommodations on the landing above the dining area. The tavern filled with a rowdy lot by the early evening, and the noise from the customers usually continued well into the night. Emmy and Sarah took most of their meals in their tiny quarters, awaiting the return of the commander in the following week. Emmy had asked the innkeeper, Edward Edween, a mousy, nosy, but proper enough cockney Brit, to query locals for any news of Northerner raiding parties and captives. The next day she told Edween to spread the word that a reward would be given for good information leading to Jacob's return. She also conveyed an interest in hiring able men should she need assistance to travel to the Tsimshian winter camp upriver.

On the fourth evening, Edween notified Emmy he had heard some rumors that might be of interest. He suggested she speak directly with the source, a trapper named Rene Marte, who occasionally passed through the region and had come into town to meet the *Pietrevos* with some trading items. Initially encouraged, Emmy noticed that Edween seemed hesitant. "You have concerns, Mr. Edween?"

The innkeeper nodded. "Yes, ma'am, I do. These are rough men, and there are stories that Marte hangs with all sorts.

And doesn't confine his trade to furs. No, ma'am. That's all I know for sure, but I believe it." He said that Marte had heard about Emmy's quest and sent word that he would visit the Red Pelican that evening.

Emmy and Sarah took dinner in the tavern main room that night and, as the pub filled with village locals—a filthy, surly lot—waited for the appearance of Marte. She noted that Sarah was fascinated with the characters and struck up a con-versation with a black robe named Tomas DeSetre, S.J., who had just come from working with the Haida on the Queen Charlottes. The priest, a Frenchman from Nance with a soft voice and sad, weary eyes, spoke of the great skill and elegant craftsmanship of the Haida people and did not believe any of the aborigines with whom he had lived could ever be respon-sible for heinous crimes. "Still, they can be childlike and, as such, quite vengeful in perceived wrongs," he noted. He gave Emmy and Sarah a blessing and told them he believed that God would watch over them, even in the most extreme of circumstances. "And may God and the Virgin keep you free from sin, especially near the moment of your death," he said.

Emmy was not pleased with this. "Father DeSetre, I don't need blessings for which I haven't asked." Embarrassed, DeSetre apologized quietly and turned back to his meal.

Sarah also introduced herself to a man at another table, a ragtag also dressed in a black robe who introduced himself as Marano Levi, a converted Jew preaching for the Jesus he had found in his world travels. He had lived in the region for three years and was convinced that the Haida were one of the lost tribes of Israel. He said he had found several passages in a well-worked Bible to recite as proof. He seemed simple and harmless enough to Emmy. She observed DeSetre watching Levi. She wondered if the disdain she saw on the Jesuit's face was from frustration at the imitation he perceived or pity for the man's soul, given that, irrespective of his baptism, he was not Catholic and therefore was likely to spend a good portion of eternity in purgatory. Levi paid no attention to the priest and ate his small meal with the fervor of a starving man, picking and eating crumbs of bread from his beard. Then he departed immediately into the darkness of the cold night. She wondered where he slept.

Marte, a small ferret of a man with pockmarked cheeks and a sharp nose that seemed fit for cutting, finally arrived, accompanied by a very tall, cachectic Negro cyclops who called himself Cull. Marte spoke quickly to Edween, watching the door and stairway during the conversation as if expecting an unpleasant interruption. Cull, however, immediately picked out Emmy and Sarah from the crowd and kept his one eye fixed on them from a perch he found by the serving bar. After the quick exchange, Marte made his way over to Emmy and Sarah and sat down without an introduction, his back to the wall, still watching the door and stairway, swinging his gaze between each entry point and then back to them. He looked over both women as if they were prizes.

Sensing a predator, Sarah moved closer to her mother as Marte spoke, yet she was fascinated at the same time with Cull, wondering how he had lost his left eye. The large rubbery scars that ran across his left brow and into his cheek had to be related to the empty socket, she surmised. She wondered if the meanness on that deformed face had preceded the painful injury, and if so, whether the anguish she perceived in him could ever be relieved. She wondered if the man had sinned to deserve the injury.

Marte addressed Emmy with darting glances while looking at Sarah. "Madame is interested in a lost boy? Perhaps one that has been taken from her soon ago? She is interested in le eschange? So I am told by Edween over there." Emmy flushed but did not respond. She leaned forward as he spoke. Sarah, losing interest in Cull, leaned forward also. Marte immediately knew he had the advantage. "It is possible to help the bereaved mother. She will barter, should a possibility exist, yes?" He quickly looked at the few wayfarers who still were in the tavern and then again at the door, then at Cull and back to Emmy. "And . . . where is the father?"

He read their faces. Smiled again. "Condolences. I lost my family in the same way when I was small like this one," he said, pointing with his chin at Sarah. Sarah reached for her mother's hand on the table. Marte saw this and changed his expression, softening for a moment. "I see this is still very painful subject. You will need some time, yes?" Then he looked over the two women again and smiled, showing his canines as he did so.

Emmy wondered what he envisioned for them, and observing the way he looked them over, saw a smile that could not hide the anger in his eyes. She sensed something painful in this little man's past, some horrible unknown thing that made him perceive himself as a victim, rationalize taking perverted pleasures at the expense of others. An opportunistic predator. She firmed up, seeing he was also surveying her wherewithal and resources. She still did not have the comfort of any official connection with the local British authorities or military and had no knowledge of the area beyond what she had learned from Edween. "Yes. We have a quest. And yes, I need more time. I am waiting for Colonel Pardeen to return from Vancouver." She saw Marte's expression change, a slight narrowing of his eyes and another quick look to the door.

"I am told the madame wishes to be guided upriver," he said, glancing at Cull. "This has been a good home. It is hard travel now. But we know this country well. The Tsimshian will be in a place called Three Spirits until the spring. They will host a potlatch, we are told, for the marriage of the tyee Ksi Amawaal's son. We will go because some of the gifts will become trade items for sale." He watched for Emmy's reaction. "Many tribes will come. Many stories." His eyes narrowed into two slits. "There may be things of interest for you there, I am feeling . . . the madame may come with us, yes?"

Emmy listened and confirmed in his expression a deep danger. She had enough information. "I will wait for the colonel."

Marte smiled and rose. "Madame may lose her one chance. The potlatch is in a fortnight. The river may be frozen, and it is a good long journey even in the summer." He looked over Emmy and then at Sarah. Smiled again at some private thought. "Bon soir, madame." He left. As he and Cull departed, Emmy saw DeSetre in the corner watching her. He shook his head and continued reading his missal.

CHAPTER TWENTY-FOUR

<><><><><><><><><><><><><><><><>

MANUITU 'STA

I t took five days for the message to reach him, but he departed immediately to meet Emmy and Sarah. MaNuitu 'sta, also known simply as "Patient River," was a tyee of the Nuxalk Bella Coola Valley clan, who, like many of the tribes along the coast, had been subjected to a swindle attempt by the Brit territorial government. Unlike most of the other leaders, however, he had not signed the treaty, and thus he had retained his stature among tribes in the region. It did not matter, however, because the whites had come anyway, swarming in from the depleted goldfields in San Francisco to make another attempt at riches in gold and coal. The resulting land disputes and differences mediated by the territorial government invariably resulted in judgments in favor of the settlers. Even then, MaNuitu 'sta had always counseled that a careful, quiet negotiation with any enemy, either the British or other tribes, brought his people better results than did angry confrontation. That moderation came as a result of learning about others and noting that a gentler approach, mastering the paths but staying out of the way of raging, intemperate actions, always seemed to win in the long life of a survivor. The Brits were here to stay, he reasoned, so it was smarter to preserve relationships and keep enemies at an observable distance rather than provoke and then justify hostile maneuvers. Early in his life, after observing the communication abilities of some of the pioneer black robe missionaries, he realized the value of assimilating languages and became conversant with all the dialects along the coast. He learned English, as well as some Russian and Spanish, and applied them to protect and enrich his clan.

Of all the tyees who had participated in the signing ceremonies, he alone had realized the discrepancies between what was being read aloud and what Antoine Bill, the Brit's hired interpreter, had conveyed to the assembled tyees. He already had a suspicion of Antoine Bill because of the Suquamish's guidance of a large contingent of bounty hunters out of Vancouver two years before that had resulted in wanton killing during a brutal takeover of Nisqually lands by coalmining settlers. But not really knowing the details of that business, MaNuitu 'sta had suspended judgment. Antoine Bill's dishonest actions during the signing ceremonies had confirmed his concerns, and he withdrew from the agreement, after unsuccessfully attempting to convince other tyees about the British deception. The Brit gifts of blankets and copper and iron utensils were enough to persuade the other elders to ignore him, with some reasoning out loud that they could always take back what they had given. A few hollered him down, embarrassing him. So he simply withdrew from the discussions. Despite that, however, he watched the ceremony, learning from it just how foolish his compatriots were.

Remaining in that encampment resulted in another event, when his youngest daughter became entranced with an American soldier, Captain George Pickett. MaNuitu 'sta had allowed his third daughter, Morning Mist, to be courted by the American, whom they all called "Pickett George." He had carefully observed Pickett and concluded he was not like the others. He also knew that Morning Mist would never be dissuaded, as stubborn as she tended to be, so he simply consented. He also presciently understood how rapidly the ways were changing, and that Morning Mist likely would fare better in a community of whites protected by a white tyee. Pickett George had proven to be reliable and fair, and he regularly sent supplies up to MaNuitu 'sta's clan. He also had traveled up north to personally deliver to MaNuitu 'sta the news of Morning Mist's death. Thus, when a message arrived with Pickett's markings asking the Bella Coola to help a woman stranger, MaNuitu 'sta did not hesitate. He was old now and needed warmth in this time of his life, so he brought one of his sons, Napen 'tjo, his youngest and brightest, to act as a guide if that became necessary.

His people, the Nuxalk, being more of an inland clan, had worked the rivers to the interior of the region as their transportation pathways and, because they were superb hunters and trappers, were intimately familiar with the lands as far north as the Stikene River. As a result, they became indispensable companions for many of the trappers who supplied the Hudson's Bay Company with furs. Over the years, they had escaped much of the internecine predation that beset peoples who lived on coastal shores. Yet they too knew about Anah and other terrors from the north. Although the Russians and many other northern raiding tribes, decimated by a series of diseases, had not waged war for over a decade, Anah had kept the fear of sudden invasions fresh enough.

Although MaNuitu 'sta was well known and was held in high regard throughout the region by whites as well as aborigines, he was not allowed to enter the fort. So, Emmy, escorted by Edween and two soldiers dispatched by the officer of the day, traveled out to meet him on a clear, flat river beach a few hundred yards beyond the front gate. As he waited, MaNuitu 'sta wondered what would compel Pickett George to make such a request. He had not asked for favors in the past. However, when he saw this Emmy, he understood—it was in her posture and in the intensity of her eyes, a way of looking that reminded him of Morning Mist—that Pickett George likely loved her and wanted to see her protected. That, he knew immediately, he could not guarantee, for she was asking to go into the dark mouth of death.

He watched the party approach, and when Emmy was ten yards away and had lifted her right hand, he extended his in the French manner and gently touched the top of her fingers, sensing, as he intended, that Emmy immediately felt a calming reassurance. He saw the young girl watching him and Napen 'tjo closely. She was a younger version of Emmy and had the same demeanor, although less reserved, but seemed just as determined as her mother.

"Pickett George is a good friend, so I came," he said to Emmy.

"Thank you. The captain told me I could rely on your help and that of the Bella Coola. You have heard of the tragedy that has befallen my family?" The sadness in his eyes told her he had heard and that he had empathy for her plight. "I need to get upriver before it freezes over, up to the Tsimshian trading winter camp, where I am told there will be a big potlatch. I believe there may be a chance to find my son there before he is traded or given as a gift. That is what I am told," said Emmy.

MaNuitu 'sta nodded and then sighed. He knew about the potlatch because word of it had spread all throughout the Tsimshian and Bella Coola regions. It would be a big event because Ksi Amawaal was very wealthy and had much pride. It might go on for ten days. He expected that several different peoples of Qualicum, Bella Bella, and Bella Coola would find their way there as a welcome break from the winter's tedium. The gossip from the ceremonies and feasts was as important as the gifts that would be given out to guests by the wealthy tyee Ksi Amawaal. He understood that many slaves likely would be present, and some would be exchanged. Were she to be so foolish as to make this journey, her appearance would need to be brief, if at all. He knew that Ksi Amawaal, a shrewd and careful negotiator who had grown fat on trading with the Bostons and Brits, would extend a mantle of protection to her while she was in his winter camp. But the presence of an unattached white woman, no matter how well protected, would disquiet the festivities and put all the peoples into a state of curiosity and agitation. And if any of the Northerners were to show up in the neutral encampment, he could not predict their actions. He tried to dissuade Emmy. She persisted.

"I will find a way to get there," she said.

He knew he had no choice in the matter. "Napen 'tjo, my son, will guide you. He is a good young man and has traveled with me. In return, I will ask a favor from you . . . that you teach him to read from this book." It was an English primer.

CHAPTER TWENTY-FIVE

◇◇◇◇◇◇◇◇◇◇◇◇◇◇◇◇◇◇◇

NAPEN 'TJO

.

His sisters and playmates called him Jojo, and he preferred that. He was born during the confused loud moments immediately after a fierce thunderstorm had torn the roof off their longhouse. In the discomfited hollering of all the clan members who were trying to secure shelter during the downpour, his cries stood out, and, because they sounded like shrill laughter, his brothers and mother also called him "Blue Jay." Although his mischievous and sometimes loud antics seemed to confirm that handle, he was intelligent and sensitive, and as he grew, he learned to adapt to situations with a discerning alacrity, repressing his innate impulse to play and jest. For he had witnessed grief.

Early on he discerned the pain that came to his family and village from the bloody disputes that sometimes erupted between clans and peoples, and, observing his father's calmer demeanor, he came to appreciate quieter solutions to disagreement rather than carrying out vendettas. Like his father, Jojo also had a keen ear for languages and could converse in many coastal dialects. But he had never learned to read the written words of any of the white languages, and thus, as competent as he knew he was in the world, he felt incomplete and disadvantaged. It was his request that MaNuitu 'sta had conveyed to Emmy. As dangerous as he knew the journey with Emmy was likely to be, it was a fair exchange. By the time the journey was over, he intended to be able to read aloud the entire primary school book to his father and family. By carrying and reading such little books, which he had been told contained the wisdom of many men, Jojo was convinced he could do anything, even sail a mighty Brit ship to the lands beyond his tribal shores.

As a little boy, Jojo had learned to imitate by watching and listening closely. When elders spoke in important gatherings, he always found a way to bring himself within hearing distance of the conversation, and afterward he delighted his sisters and brothers by repeating phrases by the various leaders with an exacting nuance and inflection. As he grew older, learned what the words meant and understood the significance of phrases, he found ways to repeat sentences out of context, frequently with hilarious applications. Thus his playmates always sought him out and begged to hear his running, imaginary dialogues between disparately motivated participants such as naïve British missionaries attempting to convert oversexed Kwakiutl squaws, or between starving hapless French trappers negotiating for dog meat with Tsimshian, who always were fat from the success of their fall hunting. Because he was always discreet with his humor, this banter was tolerated by the adults. And when he was twelve, in his father's absence, after he successfully translated a negotiation between Russian fur traders and his tribe, the tribe's elders truly came to appreciate his gifts. Over time, he was given more tasks. His confidence grew as did his curiosity and enthusiasm for newness. Jojo wanted to see the world because, he knew, it was a wonder of delight.

They were to set out in the early morning of January 20th, three days after Emmy received word that the colonel and the rest of his senior officers would not return to Fort Simpson for yet another fortnight. Jojo agreed with MaNuitu 'sta that the potlatch could likely be over by the time they negotiated and provisioned military assistance, so Emmy decided she could tarry no longer. The captain who had been left in command refused to offer any contingent to accompany Emmy and vigorously argued for her to stay and await higher authority's advice, assuring her there would be no rescue should she persist in her hardheadedness. She sent out word to acquire the services of another packer-guide and quickly arranged with Edween to outfit three sturdy canoes: one for provisions and the trading goods and two to transport her small company. She told Jojo she would bring Sarah as well because she knew she could not convince her daughter to stay behind, and Emmy sensed there was as much danger leaving Sarah behind in Fort Simpson as there would be to bring her along. There were very few women at the fort, and none appeared reputable, in her estimate. And Marte's behavior had frightened her. Jojo argued vehemently against this, noting that the girl would be a serious encumbrance and an additional temptation for slavers should they encounter them. But Emmy, thinking of Marte's leer, refused to reconsider.

The evening before they were to depart, they interviewed three men who came forward to hire for the guiding work. Jojo watched Emmy immediately dismiss the first man, handy as a carpenter by trade but also a slovenly lout with no wilderness experience and whom she believed likely would eat most of his provisions in the first few days. The second fellow had some experience as a guide but carried the external characteristics of a chronic alcoholic—a flushed red face, withered limbs, protuberant belly, and a constant fine tremor. Emmy told Jojo she had no desire to attend to a man's rum fits, which would likely appear within hours of his last drink, so she dismissed him as well. The third was Marano Levi. Despite his tattered appearance, he professed he knew the region well, having traveled it in his lonely quest to spread the Word of the Savior. And he had survived living alone in the wilderness for six years. So she hired him against Jojo's objections. Jojo was disturbed by this, despite understanding that Levi was likely the best of a weak lot, and despite the need for an extra set of hands to help them paddle the canoes. Jojo believed his own job had just been made all the more difficult by her stubborn decision. Levi was known throughout the region and was left alone by all the tribes, for he was a touched man.

It was raining lightly the next morning, and the snow from the previous week had turned into a slushy nuisance that made their transport of supplies to the canoes on the river below slow so they had some morning light silhouetting them as they pushed off. That concerned Jojo, who had wanted their departure to go unobserved. He knew that gossip might betray the small size of their party, unaccompanied as it was by any soldiers. And they had to make time. On a spring or summer day, the journey would take a week and a half at most, but in the winter, it could take three times as long if the river was frozen anywhere along its length leading to the tributary forks that defined Three Spirits. In his winter travels along the rivers in that long winding valley, Jojo had found ice obstructing canoe passage only twice, and the plateau where the Tsimshian encamped during the winter was seldom if ever snowbound. But he knew that if it was, it would be disastrous for their quest, and not just because of the dangers of the cold. Survival in a winter shelter would not be a problem, nor would the winter starvation that killed many travelers trapped by blizzards. They could forage easily. The deep rivers forming and emanating from Three Spirits were bountiful with edible life, and the winter cold made it less likely for them to encounter wolves, bear, or cougar, although he had seen plenty during this time of the year in the past. It was being late for the potlatch that would hurt them.

The first two days bode well for their passage. Jojo was pleased and told Emmy that if they made as much progress, taking them past the big gorges forty miles upstream without encountering snow, they would likely arrive a few days before the potlatch. That would give them the opportunity to meet with Ksi Amawaal and possibly have the shrewd tyee himself do the negotiating on their behalf, without the slavers knowing who was really doing the asking.

While making camp on the third day, Jojo pulled Emmy aside. "If your son is with other slaves . . . if the Northerners show up to do trading and he is with them . . . it is best that you not be seen. Because that will show them the value of your son. They may not know his family is looking for him." He saw Emmy consider her alternatives. She told him she realized that the secrecy he desired might very well have been compromised already by her own actions, for she had asked Edween to spread the word about her quest. For all she knew, she said, he might have told listeners she was a naïve, wealthy woman carrying a big reward.

Jojo went on. "Ksi Amawaal is honest, but he is also very clever, Mrs. Evers. I have watched him trade with the Brits and with trappers. He is known for always winning. He will understand the value your son brings right away. If we ask him to do so, he will take the chests you bring and all the gold you carry, consider its value, and will offer half of it to the Northerners for all their slaves, making them think he wants to give the slaves as gifts to his family and guests during the potlatch. The slavers may be insulted at the offer because they know the slaves are very valuable, but they will not fight with anyone while they are there. Ksi Amawaal will argue loudly for his position, but I have seen him do this with others—it will be a bluff." He laughed. "It will be his game, and he likes to play like this. After he calms the Northerners down, he will make them another offer, and then, to show off his wealth to all the guests and visitors during the potlatch, he will reduce what he asks. You will get your son. He will get half the gold. Everyone will see him to be a wealthy and generous tyee, and the slavers will go away thinking they have outsmarted him—but only if they do not know he is acting as a trader on your behalf."

And then, with a solemn, sad expression, Jojo said, "But if they discover us before we reach the Three Spirits, if they know you are there—carrying gold—the Northerners will come after us, kill me, and take you and your daughter as slaves. If they do not kill you too."

Jojo watch Emmy's reaction to his words. She was quiet. He saw she understood that this would be much more complicated than she had expected.

CHAPTER TWENTY-SIX

◇◇◇◇◇◇◇◇◇◇◇◇◇◇◇◇◇◇◇◇◇

JACOB AND ANAH

nah had given Little Raven the footstool he knew he deserved. Word had come from the south that he had indeed delivered the right and vengeful coup by taking the head of a grand tyee. He had also captured the tyee's only son. Understanding the value of this child, he thus held back on what he might have otherwise done to any other white captive.

There were other reasons for Anah's restraint. From the time he had defeated the big tyee and looked into his dying eyes, Anah knew he had killed one with a special magic who had bestowed a special curse upon him. Fascinated in a way he did not understand, he watched Jacob to see if he had the same power as had the tyee, his father. On the first night in safe harbor, he had brought Isaac's decaying head into the tent where Klixuatan's wife kept Jacob drugged and bound. He compared the blackening face of the trophy to Jacob's sleeping visage. He returned the next night as well, again bringing the head right next to the boy's face. And it was there—the same sweep of the brow and deep-set eyes, the determined jutting jaw, strangely similar between the grimacing movements of a child in his drugged dreams and the now exaggerated, stretched features on the trophy. The smell from the head was becoming putrid, and he would have to skin the face and scalp off soon, then tan it if he were to keep it from rotting. There would be some value to that skin, he thought. Perhaps he could seize some of the tyee's power with it.

In the cold three weeks from the time they landed by the Campbell and then moved farther north to the inland side of the channel, Anah observed Jacob as often as he could. There was something about the boy that drew his attention. Anah could not comprehend what it was, but it was related to the curse, he was certain. And thus while watching, sedentary during the healing of the deep chest wound from the death struggle with the boy's father, Anah began to think of his own early childhood, a period of his life that remained confusing to him.

He had always been ashamed that he had been unable to grow up fast enough to protect his family, and yet, he missed the happier times when he was a child, when the colors were softer. The pervasive, seething anger he felt from the time he lost his sisters had evaporated his childhood. It had disappeared like a morning fog on the water when a summer's sun first broke through the clouds.

Early on, before most men, Anah had become an adult, with all his adult appetites at once accelerated and intensified but with none of the wisdom or temperance necessary that would allow him to live safely with other men. Despite adherence to a strict warrior's discipline, taught over the years by the harsh lessons of Little Raven, Anah had never learned civil restraint because Little Raven and Klixuatan encouraged him to indulge all his passions, believing that would promote the reinvigoration of their clan. As he watched Jacob, he wondered whether this boy might grow up quickly, as he had, driven by a desperate need for survival and vengeance. Was this boy a replica of himself? Was this somehow part of the curse?

On the fifteenth day of Jacob's captivity, Klixuatan gradually began reducing the drugs. He untethered Jacob two days later and, with Anah, watched to see if the boy would flee. He did not. Still, Klixuatan and Anah continued watching the boy, unsettled, for Klixuatan had observed what Anah had seen. He understood that Jacob had a smoldering fire in him, which the shaman feared was likely ready to burst forth if left uncontained. In the hours after his capture, the boy had fought so vigorously that Klixuatan had had to strike him repeatedly and then bind him tightly to try to stop him from provoking retribution from others. Several of the men now referred to him as "Little Wolverine" because of the painful bites and scratches Jacob had given them. One warrior's deep bite marks from Jacob had festered despite the poultices the shaman had applied. Drugging Jacob was the only thing that had worked to keep the boy down. Klixuatan would have killed any other child with such venom. But he knew about the curse the boy's father had made on Anah. Killing the boy would only make it worse. They had to contain him.

Jacob was watching them also. As his delirium dispersed and his exhaustion diminished, he began to understand his dilemma. And then, after looking without success for the other boy he had seen in the tent on the journey up the sound, he realized he was the lone white in the encampment. He became aware of the difference between those who were enslaved and those who had the freedom to move about freely. But the difference was more than the tethers; it was the depressed countenances and fearful actions that distinguished the captives when they were spoken to by others. And they never fought back when pushed or shoved. On one of the few times he saw any resistance from one of the slaves—a heavily tattooed young woman who looked the same age as his Aunt Corrie— he saw her receive a severe beating that left her in a bloodied mess. After the beating, the old crone, Klixuatan's woman, who had been in the boat with him, went to her and helped her up, berating the woman while she administered water and covered her with a blanket. When the slave pushed Klixuatan's woman away and angrily spit out several bloody teeth at her, he saw the shaman stand and quietly walk over, pull the hapless captive's head back by the hair, and cut her nose off right down to the flat of her face. After witnessing that,

Jacob kept quiet. And he watched. In the night, shivering in the tent under a lean-to that looked like it had been present for many seasons, he thought back over the events that had brought him here—a dark passage—and he was alone. With each breath, his ribs hurt from the kicks he had received from one of the men he had bitten. He held himself from coughing to avoid the stabbing pains beneath a deep black bruise on his right side. For two days after that beating, his pee was dark brown.

Despite all that he had seen, Jacob told himself he was not afraid. At first, he tried not to look at the line of rotting heads impaled on tall poles surrounding the encampment, placed there, he realized, to protect the tribe from enemies and keep its slaves trapped inside. But after a few days, he was able to look up at the totems. And on the fourth day, he forced himself to consider the features of the spiked head closest to his tent. It was covered with flies and maggots, and much of the skin and deeper flesh had been eaten away, exposing all the teeth on the left side of the face. The hair was a silky black and straight, short enough that it must have been a man's head. From his tent, he stared at it for a long time.

The next day, he walked up to each of the other heads, ten in all, and studied each of them, each one in a different state of decomposition. All were that of males, but he could not tell their ages or their races, except for the three that had beards, the heads of white settlers most likely. The head he thought he had seen when they had first landed—the one that looked like his father's—was not among them. It had to have been a dream. His father was too strong and great a fighter to have succumbed, he tried to reassure himself.

Jacob watched and knew he was being watched by everyone in the camp. He saw that the big warrior who had the chest bandage had to be their tyee, for when that man spoke or gestured, everyone turned to him, some stooped, and a few cowered. Jacob felt contempt for them. He wasn't going to be afraid of that man.

And every night he reached into his pocket and felt for the reassurance of the small collection of treasures that had been there the day he was captured. He pulled them out when he was sure he was alone, reexamining them one by one: a piece of sand-polished blue glass from the beach near his home, the beak of a downed eagle he had found one day while walking with Sarah, a lead musket ball his father had given him while molding bullets, and a small ball of multicolored twine with a hundred knots tying the bits and pieces together. That reoriented him, and with that nightly exercise, he found the courage to resist.

He was not going to be afraid of that man. He was not going to be afraid of the old woman or the old man either. Or any of them. He knew he could escape when the right moment came. And if any of them had hurt his father or any of his family—the flush and anger built up and made him breathe so fast that he got dizzy—he would kill them. "I will kill them," he told himself repeatedly.

Four days later, a southern Kwakiutl trading party canoed into the encampment. Little Raven had always been careful to keep raids away from these particular Kwakiutl villages—a prudent decision because more than once the Kwakiutl had given him important information as well as valuable outlets for trade. After exchanging lead, powder, and sugar, the traders told Anah about the off-season Tsimshian potlatch up the Skeena River. Ksi Amawaal, a wealthy and powerful tyee, had extended a generous and broad invitation to surrounding tribes, they told him. They also told him that the family of a white tyee from the south was seeking a kidnapped child and was asking questions at the British fort.

Anah knew the danger inherent in making a long trip upriver, but enough trading would occur in that gathering that he could exchange slaves for many things. Still, he would have to be careful to disguise himself as Kwakiutl or Skidegate. It would be unlikely that he would be recognized, in any case, because almost all his predation had been against coastal villages. And he knew that enslaved humans were commodities that had never lost their value. Even after the Brits and French had stopped directly authorizing any form of slavery by their citizenry, they ignored the practice of slave trading by nonwhites in the region, thus condoning its continued use as a currency.

He would make this trip up into the Tsimshian country, Anah decided. Come spring, when he could rendezvous with intermediaries like Marte and Cull, who had a convenient connection to ocean-bound buyers, a raid into the south Puget Sound waters again would bring him enough women to buy another cannon. He would make this trip. And he would bring his slaves with him, including the Little Wolverine boy, if he could keep him contained.

CHAPTER TWENTY-SEVEN

◇◇◇◇◇◇◇◇◇◇◇◇◇◇◇◇◇◇◇

EMMY

Emmy was not afraid of the cold. Each winter, passed over the years under the dull and sulking skies of the Oregon territory, had presented to her new problems that she had to contain quickly. She knew that if she did not prepare properly, the deterioration of everything touched by the withering, relentless rain would deplete her strength and ultimately run her down and over. She had watched others succumb. But she repeatedly had succeeded in besting the challenges of the elements, had endured because she held to hope and purpose—and that process had hardened her to the perennial coming of the cold, personified in her mind as a wretched and angry misanthropist. And when she reemerged into its presence, when its piercing, aching grasp reintroduced itself to her fingers and nose and cut to her core, she was prepared to defiantly withstand and survive. And on the cold came that week, seven days into their trek east, first with a flurry of pea-sized hail that started in the early afternoon, followed by a torrent of freezing rain that lasted all night. The rain turned to snow by morning, stuck quickly, and within a few hours was four inches deep.

Emmy listened with considerable anxiety to Jojo's recommendation that they prepare to wait. She did not want to lose time. She needed to find Jacob. She knew he would be there. And Marano Levi had said the weather was usually milder in the protected valley of Three Spirits.

Jojo scoffed at Levi's recommendation to move on upstream. "If the weather stops us, it will do the same to others who are coming east," he reasoned. "We have to stay here at least until the snow stops. If it doesn't get cold again, we can go on." But the snow continued for another day, and then a cold hard freeze set in. Ice began to form on the river below their camp so they stayed put, going through half of their provisions in the next week.

On the second day, Jojo, anticipating a long and boring wait, brought the primer to Emmy for his first lesson. He opened the book and pointed to the pictures of common objects with their titles on the first few pages. "Raven?" he asked.

Emmy shook her head. "No. Bird," she said, pointing to the word.

"Noburd," Jojo repeated.

Emmy shook her head again. "Bu-ir-da." Jojo nodded and repeated, "Buirda." Emmy smiled and nodded. "Bird!"

Jojo repeated the word with the exact emphatic affirmative intonation. And then Emmy knew that Jojo was a perfect mimic. Within a few hours, Jojo had mastered five pages of pictures and script.

Every night and into the bitter mornings, Emmy dreamed. One night she found herself in bed waiting for someone to come through her door, and she knew it wasn't Isaac. She waited for whomever he was to be bold enough to push his way in. In the morning, she ran outside and buried her face in the snow to calm herself before Sarah awakened. Sometimes she was following a spirit who looked like a version of her first husband, Sarah's father, a hard-pressing, driven man who had changed from charming to angry within a few months after arriving in Olympia.

"Why did you marry the man who was Sarah's father?" Jojo had asked the night before, as they huddled around the small campfire. She had responded that she didn't really know why. She was fifteen when the man had come into town to raise money for a speculative enterprise in the far Northwest—one that would bring huge fortunes to down-in-their-luck Boston brownstone legatees whose patrimony was meager, most of whom believed in getting something for nothing. He told of an enterprise involving San Francisco provisions in exchange for Northwest gold, furs, and lumber. He was a good storyteller and painted a grand vision, and she had been swept away by the romance of living in a foreign, savage land. He had fooled Emmy all the way, and yet she stayed with him, even as they became more estranged. She recalled her mother's advice—to always marry someone much older, preferably a man who was beyond roaming eyes, or to at least be young enough that the possibility of being replaced by someone younger yet would be a remote threat.

In a short time after their marriage, Emmy's husband became violent, never turning on her but on others, and she experienced a growing, despairing loneliness much stronger than the frustrated solitude that had driven her into his arms in the first place. By her pregnancy with his child she had faintly hoped for a softening, but it did not come. And then he was dead—taken on a very muggy morning when, as it turned out, all she could think about was how mistaken she had been to marry that man and how much more foolish it was to be continuing in that relationship. But she had felt no guilt. It just was Providence's answer to unasked prayers. "I don't know why I married him," she told Jojo.

"Why did you marry Jacob's father?" asked Jojo.

"Because I loved him," she said after a pause. "That is something I am trying to understand now that he is gone— why it doesn't hurt more. But as we lived through our time together . . ." She looked up and saw that Sarah was awake and listening. She looked at Jojo and shook her head. She had said enough of her private thoughts to this young man whom she believed would never understand. They watched the fire quietly for a while. Then she turned the inquiry on him. "Tell me about Captain Pickett. And your sister."

Jojo looked at her and blushed. "She was beautiful, like you and your daughter," he said. "She was fifteen, like you say you were when you moved away from the Boston-Man land. Maybe she wanted to get away, see new things like you did. She came home one time with him when she was with child. I never saw her again."

"What was she like?" asked Sarah.

"We played when we were young," he said. "She knew how to do things, climb a big tree and catch a small bird on the perch, just for a moment, and let it fly again. She taught me to do that. I made her laugh, and she made me want to make her laugh because it was such a pretty laugh. She loved Pickett George very much."

"Did Pickett George love her?" asked Sarah.

Jojo saw how closely Emmy was listening. Looking away from her, he nodded his head. "Yes."

That night Emmy dreamed of riding on a horse next to Pickett George. They were going someplace important. Inspecting. He wore his field cape and sword and stayed at an even pace with her.

On the fifth night, she listened to Marano Levi talking to himself, walking through the snow in the darkness away from the campfire they shared for dinner. He was chanting an obscure Catholic office in Latin. When he was out of earshot, Jojo repeated the entire vesper perfectly and then cackled in delight when he received a chastising look from Sarah. The laughter was so disarming that Sarah's disapproval evaporated. When Levi the chanter returned to camp a short while later, Jojo spoke to him in the exact same tenor, imitating with the perfect nuance of Levi's ramblings. Emmy saw a conspiratorial glance pass between Sarah and Jojo, but Levi did not seem to notice. Then she saw Sarah turn to Levi and, after a brief pause, speak to him with some concern and a tinge of tender affection. "You know, Marano, you will catch your death out there in this cold. Please have some of this potage." Marano continued his chanting for a few more minutes, seeming to ignore the offer, but then closed his missal and quietly sat down next to Sarah. She put a bowl of hot soup into his hands. There was no more talking in the camp that night.

On the ninth day, it began to rain again, melting away the snow and much of the ice. On the tenth, the sun came out and the sky stayed blue all day. And then the next. So they prepared to strike camp. Emmy and Sarah moved with an anxious urgency. Too much time had been lost.

CHAPTER TWENTY-EIGHT

<><><><><><><><><><><><><><><><><><>

MARANO LEVI

Marano Levi was born Ignatio Hortensio Ramonez-Basillon into a family of clever, multitalented Castilian merchants. As a fifth son, however, he was penniless after the death of his father, so he knew at a young age that his opportunities were limited to serving at the beneficence of his oldest brother, an arrogant man who showed little kindness. Although he had been baptized as Catholic, as had three previous generations before him, the young Ignatio learned by chance, while looking through old ledgers in his grandmother's house, the secret that his family was, in fact, Hebrew, with the surname Levi. This hidden stigma made him sensitive to the words he heard in church, equally condemnatory of Jews and Muslims, and by the time he turned fourteen, he had developed a painful resentment of his family and its history of capitulation to the deadly ultimatums of the Castilian Catholic clergy. Increasingly critical of what he perceived as an ignorant cowardice, he left home for the new world, cursed by his family for abandoning his obligation to subservience. As he walked the streets of Castile for the last time, he decided he would adopt the ancient Levi family surname and thereafter call himself "Marano," which was a term reserved by the Castilians for Jews who covertly maintained their Christ-killer heritage. The curse bestowed on him by his family increased his resolve to never return to the repressed, dark, and angry milieu of that small hilltop home.

He walked all the way to Barcelona, determined to make a new life for himself. After a year of enterprising hard work, he saved enough to buy passage on a trading ship to Veracruz, Mexico. There he applied his energy and bargaining skills, again saving carefully so that he might ultimately purchase his own land to farm north in the rich and fertile American Texas territory. Before he could save enough to do so, however, he found himself conscripted along with thousands of less industrious but equally hapless men into Santa Anna's new army. He could not buy his way out from the servitude. Fortunately, because he had learned to cook in Spain and could do many other things well—such as repair shoes, tame horses, and cut beautiful carvings from the abundant indigenous mesquite— he caught the attention of one of Santa Anna's staff orderlies and became a valued member of the generalissimo's officers' camp. That was a comfortable position, and within a few months, Marano had been promoted to the rank of corporal. The advantage proved short-lived, for a few weeks later the entire army began a long, exhausting forced march to northern Mexico to confront Winfield Scott's American army. Five thousand men perished in that brutal trek across the barren plains of central Mexico, and an exhausted army prepared itself for battle against a smaller but well-equipped and well-fed American force.

In the battle of Cerro Gordo, as the result of a brilliant tactical exploration by a young captain named Robert E. Lee, Winfield Scott's dragoons flanked Santa Anna, forcing the Mexican hidden artillery to fire prematurely, revealing their positions to Scott's frontal assault forces. Scott thereby successfully flushed Santa Anna's well-ensconced army from a high-ground position, and panic turned to bloody pandemonium. With his defeated army in disarray, Santa Anna narrowly escaped, leaving behind in his haste all his personal effects, including his best wooden leg—one which Marano had been entrusted to repair. Seizing this as his only opportunity to survive a merciless slaughter, Marano stripped off his uniform and, speaking in the wayfarer English he had taught himself while working in a Veracruz cantina, showed the ornately carved prosthesis to a young Illinois lieutenant. Thus, carrying the carving held high before him, Marano was escorted through the American lines to the headquarters of Scott, to whom he surrendered the trophy. In the confused jubilation of the victorious American camp, Marano was able to make his way out of the territory, safely distancing himself from both armies.

A week later, riding a wild mustang he had lassoed, he crossed the Rio Grande and wisely kept heading north, thus avoiding the Comanche territory he knew many Mexican army refugees would attempt to transverse. When he reached the Missouri River, he attached himself to a wagon train headed west for California, where gold had been discovered. His luck changed there again—for while working atop a flagpole during a tempestuous San Francisco spring storm, he was struck by lightning. He remained in a coma for three weeks, cared for by two Irish Catholic Dominican nuns who saw the incident and, finding papers on him that identified him as Marano Levi, apostate Jew, baptized him back into Christianity. When he awoke, he was mostly deaf and had forgotten all but his name and some of the native Spanish he had known as a child. Thus he began his life anew as Marano Levi, Christian convert.

The nuns developed great affection for Marano and watched over him as best they could, providing him with tasks and an allowance that would sustain him. But they worried about his ability to survive on his own, for although he seemed intelligent enough when focused on a task, he was constantly distracted by small fits that left him for several minutes with a trance-like staring affect. He never was observed in a conniption, but more than once he was robbed during the quiet seizure. None of their prayers, poultices, or incantations cured him. During such episodes, he just stopped functioning altogether. The nuns even tried a concoction provided by a well-regarded Chinese herbalist, who told them it would work only if Marano took the expensive mixture twice a day for several weeks. He did so but without success; in fact, the fits seemed to increase in frequency.

When their order reassigned them to move from San Francisco, the sisters arranged for Marano to be attached to the service of an aging, frail French Jesuit missionary who needed an assistant for a mission assignment to convert aborigines in the savage Vancouver territory. Six months later, Marano Levi made his way north with the black robe. The pair traveled together for eighteen months, and during that time, Marano seldom spoke. He observed carefully, however, and came to understand his master's compulsive devotion to Jesus. The priest awoke every morning before dawn, said his Mass, prayed for an hour afterward, ate a meager breakfast, then proceeded to travel, visiting the camps of tribes friendly enough to receive them and avoiding ones that had reputations. Marano respected this routine and became devoted to it as well.

At the end of their eighteenth month together on the northwestern shore of Vancouver Island, the priest began coughing. Overcome during the cold night with shaking chills, by morning he could not rise from his pallet. There was no one to send for. The priest was dead by evening. At first, Marano continued with his normal tasks: hunting, fishing, and trapping for two mouths to feed as he always had. But by the third day, overwhelmed by the putrefaction in the tent, he buried the priest. The next morning, after a prolonged seizure that left him disoriented and messed, he found himself preparing for the Mass in the same manner as he had done for the past two years. When he regained his senses, he changed out of the soiled clothing and donned the priest's cassock. As he emerged from the tent, he was confronted by three aborigines. They pointed muskets at him and, after gathering up the chalice and makeshift altar, motioned him to their canoe. Their tyee, Tsa ka tien', was dying.

The trip to the chieftain's lodge became another starting place for Marano. After ministering as best he could to the elderly chief and applying an improvised extreme unction rite, Marano Levi began a new vocation as a vagrant unordained priest, performing the semblance of a Mass and, for the families that would allow him to do so, baptizing their newborn and anointing with last rites their gravely ill. In his wanderings through the region over the next three years, he memorized a tattered Spanish Bible and, interpreting passages randomly, became convinced that the aborigines of Vancouver Island were one of the lost tribes of Israel, his "Infantes desperadoes des Juda." He was inspired by repeated epiphanies, usually occurring right after a prolonged seizure, and understood in a way no one else could that God was all around and in every living twig and hard stone. He accepted as revelation that his mission was to convert all creatures into a harmonious peace. He was passionate about his beliefs and deeply confused most of the time, speaking in a hodgepodge of English, French, Spanish, and Chinook to whomever would listen. And because his ceremonies were a spectacle of incantations and improvised motions that infuriated any clergy, Protestant or Catholic, who happened to witness them, word spread. Within a short time, he was shunned. The natives left him alone, and Marano Levi became a lonely and depressed shepherd without a flock. It was in that state of mind that he found himself in the camp of Emmy Evers.

CHAPTER TWENTY-NINE

EMMY, SARAH, AND URSA

The snow rapidly melted over the next few days under an unusually warm winter sun. Jojo ordered the small band to break down camp in preparation for an early morning departure and asked Marano to hunt and fish to replenish their meat supplies. In the late afternoon light, while Jojo disassembled the supply tent and packed the third canoe, Sarah and Emmy started foraging for dry wood for the night fire.

◇◇◇◇◇◇◇

They were not alone in the forest. One hour before, as the late afternoon soft wind changed direction and drifted in from the water and up the hills, it had carried with it the complex smell of a downed animal. A few miles away, a grizzly had picked up the scent and immediately moved south to the water, pushing with his big shoulders through dense undergrowth of decayed blackberry vines. Other bear and wolves would be on it soon, and the grizzly knew it might have to fight again. This was an older bull bear that had survived every violent encounter over its many years, always emerging bolder and more confident. Big by comparison to other grizzly in the region, it needed to feed constantly. Lean from a short hibernation, it had emerged from its den starving the week before, and since then, it had been unable to find much prey. There were few fish in the stream. The bear knew it had to get to the dead animal first, before other predators. Last fall just before hibernation, the grizzly had been in a fight with an angry wolverine over the carcass of a moose. The disagreeable animal just wouldn't back down and had scraped a gash through the grizzly's right eye before the grizzly had found just the right position and swatted the wolverine with such force that it flew against a big cedar and did not get up again. The bear gorged itself on the moose and wolverine and then settled down to sleep. When it emerged from hibernation, it could not see from its right eye, and since then, the fighting was so much more work.

Most of the fallen timber was wet, but as Emmy and Sarah moved up a deer trail, they entered a cove with so much canopy cover that it had been protected from the snow that still blanketed much of the area. While Sarah laid out a drag cloth to tow the wood, Emmy began stacking semidry branches into a neat pile on the cloth. When she returned to it with a third armful, she saw a tree stump move. But it wasn't a tree at all. When the massive bear stood up onto its hind legs, it appeared as big as a mountain. Sarah's back was to the bear, and when she looked up, she saw that her mother had stopped still, staring past her. Sarah did not turn. Both of them could hear the heavy breathing of the grizzly. Emmy held tightly onto the branches of dry wood she carried. But not tightly enough. A heavy piece slipped, then dropped and deflected off her knee onto the ground. The huge old silver-back, hovering over the decomposing remains of an elk cow, turned to the sound, and as it did so, Emmy saw that its mouth was full of bloody carrion. The wind was with them, and it was close enough that she could smell the foul dung on its hide and see that one eye was missing. The bear sniffed the air, sensing for the presence of an intruder. From the way it turned its ears and moved its head, Emmy knew it had not placed them yet. She motioned to Sarah with her eyes and carefully began stepping backward, looking for a pathway for them to escape unimpeded. When the grizzly turned its good eye away from her, she dropped her bundle and began running, whispering loudly, "Run, Sarah. To the camp." The beast turned and saw the movement. Bellowing, it dropped to all fours. Sarah screamed in a high-pitched shrill that crescendoed over the low roar of the grizzly, which had begun rushing toward the fleeing women. As it broke through the saplings over the ridge they had crossed, the women saw movement and a flash of light off to the right. The bear shuddered from the pain of a bullet striking its shoulder. As the bear turned toward the flash, standing fully upright and roaring loudly, Emmy and Sarah continued running in the direction of camp.

When Emmy looked back, she saw Marano Levi fifty feet away from the roaring beast. He was hurriedly reloading his musket for a second shot. But the bear, wounded and furious, leaped the short distance in four quick, bounding strides and knocked the man to the ground. It bit into Marano's jaw and head. The dull, crunching sound and screams of the dying man carried loudly through the forest. Emmy and Sarah cried out in horror. This time the bear caught their scent and turned away from Marano. It charged after them, running parallel toward the river below. Emmy broke through the trees on the riverbank first and saw a canoe beached on its side. "Get to that boat, Sarah!" The bear came through the trees sixty yards upstream. She saw it stand and sniff the air, catching their scent again. Just as they reached the vessel, it roared and charged up through the shoals toward them. The women put the boat between themselves and the animal. The canoe's gunnels were high enough that the bear could not cross over it and, as the animal started to move around the prow to reach the other side, they both leaped into the boat. From the opposite side, the bear crawled into the boat as well, and as it did so, its massive weight swung the craft into the water. The canoe started downstream carrying the three of them with it. As Sarah and Emmy, still screaming, started to jump from the boat, they heard two loud reports and saw the big bear suddenly drop headfirst into the water. It did not move again, and its weight held the canoe fixed in the shallow part of the stream. Two men emerged from the woods, each carrying a smoking fifty-caliber rifle. It was Marte and Cull.

"Ze girls is playing hide-and-go-seek with the big beast, eh?" Marte said. Cull, making his way over to the bear with a drawn knife to finish it if necessary, exhaled a deep, coarse bass cackle at Marte's joke.

Moments later, Jojo found them. As he silently approached the canoe, he surveyed the dead grizzly and then Marte and his companion. Taking in the smug grins of the shooters and with hands on his knives, Jojo stepped between the men and the two women. Marte smiled. Doffing his filthy fur hat, he bowed deeply toward Emmy as if he were mimicking the formal address to royalty. "You are most welcome, madame." Brushing aside his sarcastic display, Emmy wondered to herself what this might cost them.

They found Marano Levi's broken body and spent the rest of the afternoon burying him in the cold, hard ground. Jojo put the Spanish Bible in the lonely man's grave. Although it was not a lucky book, Jojo said he knew it had given Marano some comfort in this world and might help him find his way in the next.

CHAPTER THIRTY

MARTE, CULL, AND EMMY

In the hour preceding total darkness, Cull had skinned and quartered the grizzly. "Mus bin fi'teen hunded pouns, all tol," he said, stretching the skin onto a makeshift rack. He held out a long strip of bear backstrap to Emmy and Sarah and leered with a jack-o'-lantern grin when Sarah grimaced and then shuddered. "Sted it eat yo, yo eaten' it," he said, and then put the strip of flesh into his mouth. Marte smiled at Sarah's reaction.

Jojo knew of Rene Marte. The trapper had established himself in the Nuxalt and the Skeena River area as an opportunistic intermediary between white non-English-speaking traders and various coastal tribes, including the Kwakiutl and, it was rumored, the more predatory of the northern raiders. Somewhere, in the past few years, Jojo surmised, Marte had picked up Eben Cull as a running companion. Although Jojo had never seen that grim giant before, he had heard of him and knew he was a cold murderer with a reputation that seemed a fitting complement to that of the unctuous Frenchman. The Brits were without warrant for him and, as thinly garrisoned as they were, had no time to hunt Cull in any case. They simply ignored the rumors. No citizens would have been bold enough to bring any concerns forward because the frontier had just too many similar denizens, and the consequences of exercising one's citizenship were precarious. Most knew that murderers like Cull and Marte were swift to deliver preemptive violence, and everyone knew about revenge as a prime motivator for those who lived on the periphery.

Emmy realized to be in the debt of these men for the rescue from the bear was a horrible conundrum that further complicated her quest. Both she and Jojo knew their lives were in danger, particularly if it was true that Marte and Cull were slavers. Enslavement was far worse than death, she had decided long ago.

That night she insisted that Jojo sleep in the same tent with the trading goods and with her and Sarah. But only Sarah slept. Jojo kept his muskets fully cocked, and Emmy loaded the pepperbox's six barrels and capped the primers on the weapon's nipples. Emmy hadn't lain this close to any man other than her husbands, and she would have been embarrassed in other circumstances. But she knew there was imminent danger from the new visitors, so she huddled close to Jojo and Sarah all night. The warmth and their weapons helped, and Emmy nodded off.

In those few minutes, she plunged deeply into a dream, and she was back on Whidbey in her own bed and the wind howled outside. She reached over with her foot feeling for Isaac's warmth as she had when they first were married, and he would let her place her cold, small feet on the broad dorsum of his so she could push herself up high enough to kiss him. But that had stopped when he returned from the Indian war, as had all of the tenderness in their intimate moments. She found herself during that brief dream longing for that. But she couldn't find Isaac, and when she snagged her healing toe on a rent in one of the hides, the pain startled her. She remembered where she was and stayed awake the rest of the night.

Morning finally came—another clear blue sky, unseasonably warm. When they emerged from their tent, they saw Cull down by the river packing his canoes. One held several barrels of whiskey among other containers. Marte was seated directly outside, waiting, smiling slyly at them as he drilled into a huge bear canine that would eventually become part of a necklace. His expression conveyed amusement, either for their precautions or for a projected intimacy between Emmy and Jojo. In either case, his tone barely concealed contempt. "Madame would like the services of guardians into the gathering?" he asked. Emmy waited. Hearing no response, he went on. "I am told there will be many of the peoples of this region at this potlatch. I am told there will be visitors there who very well may have what you seek. I know them. I know them well."

Emmy looked over at Jojo for some direction. "We will speak directly with Ksi Amawaal," Jojo said. His hand was on his knife. "He is expecting us," he lied. Marte considered this, sneered dismissively, and rose. When Emmy did not correct Jojo's assertion, Marte spat onto the ground.

"As you wish." Marte walked down to the canoe and spoke briefly to Cull, then returned. "You will have no objections if we move upriver to the potlatch with you? It is dangerous in these parts," he said and laughed to himself. "Everyone comes to these potlatches looking for something. And everyone departs with something."

And so they moved upstream, keeping Marte and Cull visible in front of them but far enough away that a musket shot from them would be difficult. Jojo and Emmy both paddled, while Sarah sat in the second canoe and kept watch on the other tow-behind. They were all nervous about their new company. Emmy had concealed the gold in a small chest under several skins. The rest of the gifts—copper, iron, glass, several beautifully polished and semiprecious stones, fine lace, various small implements such as a large assortment of thimbles, and nails in gross bundles—were individually wrapped in linen or buckskin. But it wasn't their belongings that concerned them. Marte and Cull were desperate, despicable men, unpredictable and without honor. Jojo told Emmy that, when they arrived at the Three Spirits Valley sometime next week, they must somehow find their way to Ksi Amawaal before Marte and Cull could mingle into the festivities. The two trappers would certainly expose their presence to the Northerners if they arrived first. Jojo knew he had to immediately invoke Ksi Amawaal's protection for the women.

Emmy was exhausted from a sleepless night. While paddling, after seeing that Sarah had fallen asleep in the canoe behind and could not hear, she asked Jojo about Marte and Cull. "I am told that Marte came from a place they call 'Keybeck,' far east of here," Jojo said. "He arrived in this region twelve years ago, and I remember seeing him when I was a little boy. He traded furs and other things to men on the ships, and my father said he always had information about every deal that went on all around. That's what I remember." Jojo paddled for a while, then continued. "For a short time, he traveled with old Antoine Bill, a Suquamish who translated for the King George Men. When Antoine Bill finally got himself killed because he lied one too many times, that Marte fella tried doing translation in Chinook. But he wasn't very good at most of the people's words. So I am told he went on to other things.

"As for Cull, I don't know much about that man except that he carries two big knives and eats his meat raw. He is mean like a poked dog. You saw him last night. I know about two gold diggers from a place called Bama who argued with him one night. They both disappeared a few days later. They never came back for their grubstakes, so many thought he killed them. If so, nobody ever found their bodies . . . Some say he ate them."

Emmy shuddered. She felt for the pepperbox in her cloak, hoped the powder was dry. Furious at the inept, rule-bound Brit captain who had refused to send men, she ran her thumb over the hammer, seeking some assurance from the weapon. She had come to understand the Americans' reasons for declining. They might be facing down the Brits right now . . . and maybe that's why the Brits hadn't returned to their post at Fort Simpson. She thought about the first time she saw Pickett, and it strangely stirred her—but she could not afford to hold on to that thought . . . dismissed it with the feeling that she was stronger than him . . . but knew, insecure as she sensed he was at his core, that he was probably an efficient killer like so many of the military she had met over the years . . . and wished that she could have had George Pickett with them right now. In the presence of killers, it didn't matter if someone who was on your side was a good person, just that he was calm and competent.

She wished that Isaac had not gotten himself killed. That thought made her angry with him, and then, holding back a shiv-like piercing that went to her chest and caught her breath, she was angry with herself. Isaac always had been so noble and so foolish—and so taken with her as he was that he always did what he thought she wanted. But he had not understood her, and that had kept her isolated in a way that added a blue dimension to everything she did, all year round, an enveloping wrap that couldn't be broken by comforts or reassurances. She thought about the conundrum that comes when one has reached the thin boundary between love and hatred, and how impatience bridged the gap between those two very deep emotions. She thought to herself how swiftly a person moved from the blindness of love and admiration to the clouded emotions of contempt and hatred. She had never crossed over into hatred for Isaac in the way she had with her first husband. She just had grown tired of reassuring Isaac constantly and picking up after his messes, quietly accepting the societal dictum that gave all credit to the male in the relationship. They had created an unacknowledged partnership, but he had never really given her equality in it. His pride had been too great to acknowledge it, even in private with her, and that, in its finality, was what she resented most in him. She had accepted that with equanimity but, by the time he had left to fight Indians east of the mountains, she had come to an uneasy conclusion about the fairness of their relationship. And when she was given the opportunity to manage the estate, she embraced it with a hungry vengeance, and it all prospered as it never had before.

She had been disappointed, she realized, when Isaac had returned. And things were different ever after that. She thought about cowards like Tom Iserson, who had jumped out of the window that night, naked, leaving everyone behind. Fitting it was, that naked state, for the imbecile he was. Then he had the gall to tell people that he had "held the door to keep the killers at bay" while everyone else escaped. She felt herself getting hot, and then the cold breeze evaporated the fluster. So many men were cowards like that—pathetic partners to women who had even less backbone. Fortunately, most of those partnerships did not survive for long out here, unprotected by the well-meaning conventions of a civilized society that believed there was a place for everyone.

As she paddled quietly, Emmy thought about this foolish

fix she had gotten herself and Sarah into. She watched Jojo and hoped he was as smart and skillful as he seemed. He was earnest and wise, far beyond his years, and had a keen instinct that allowed him to assess every situation quickly and correctly, yet he also had the manners to allow her to retain a sense of control. She had learned by watching him and how he approached each decision and crisis, saw how he anticipated problems and found alternatives that averted crisis in the first place. She knew she could enhance that skill in herself and, if she survived, carry it forward in whatever new life she would create for herself afterward. After she achieved her driven mission to find Jacob before he was destroyed—and if she survived.

She thought about the last time she had seen Jacob, running from the savages, the same ones she was hoping to meet up with somehow. To make a fair trade . . . if they understood that. She was applying a very quaint interpretation to that concept, she realized, and the reality was that it would be defined in the end by something deep down that most did not understand, an instinct that ran through everything around her—survival, with all negotiations bound together by hope on both sides of the bargain. Understanding what the other side needed was the real problem. And in this situation, she had brought material goods and gold but doubted that was what the aborigines really were after. Was it hope for something beyond material gain? What was it they really wanted? She shook her head and realized that a very simple set of hopes was the only bright thing that Marte had brought—with word that Jacob really might be at Three Spirits. For that, at least, she was thankful. For a brief night, it had allowed her to nod asleep in an exhausted heap—briefly, but deeply—with dreams about finding her family, as perfectly imperfect as they were together, the way they were the day before it was destroyed.

Jojo knew she was worried. "These two have not made a move, Missus Evers. Yet. But Marte is thinking about it. They don't know what we carry. Marte thinks we are more valuable to them just as we are because he will try to become an adviser to the Northerners if they are there—to give them an advantage. He is thinking that when all offers have been put on the table, if an exchange does occur, if Jacob is there, he can find us for the Northerners and they can take Jacob back, kill me, and take you and Sarah. Marte is thinking he will get something from this and maybe it is safer to wait to see. Besides, he has whiskey to sell, and that will take up much of his time. It is after the exchange that will be the most dangerous. Getting you all back alive." They spoke no more for several hours.

Late that afternoon they were joined by a party in three other small cedar dugouts. "Tsimshian," said Jojo, who spoke to them briefly as they moved alongside and kept pace for a short distance before peeling off into a tributary. Because Emmy and Sarah had wrapped themselves in blankets, covered their heads with reed knit hats, and darkened their faces with mud as Jojo had insisted, they were not noticed, or at least the other canoeists paid no attention to them. "They said Three Spirits is only a long half-day from here," Jojo said, watching Marte and Cull pull to shore, presumably to camp.

"We will be there in the morning if we make our camp here, but if we keep moving, we will be there after dark tonight. That is what I think we should do. Let Marte think we are camping downstream and then move ahead in the dark." He looked up into the sky. "No moon tonight. That is good, but we will need to be careful." They pulled ashore and started as if to make camp.

Five hours later, quietly, carefully still-paddling against a slowly moving current, Jojo, Emmy, and Sarah passed the sleeping killers and moved upstream. Within five more hours, they could see campfires and massive longhouses. They had entered Three Spirits.

CHAPTER THIRTY-ONE

<<<<<<<<<<<<<<<<<<>>>>>>

SARAH

S he had wept bitterly as they buried Marano, even more so than when they had put her stepfather into the ground. Isaac had left with a heroic reputation that would keep him alive for many, and that had comforted her. But Marano was a different kind of hero. Sarah had developed a fondness for the lonely man that made her feel almost motherly. He had been such a lost soul, she thought, so misunderstood. No one had bothered to try to understand Marano Levi. In his final act when he shot the beast, he was more focused than she had ever seen him during the short time he had been with them. And the teasing to which Jojo had subjected him was mean, but it seemed to not affect

Marano. She concluded that beset as he was by his seizures, Marano nevertheless had found a place of peace in his life. It was a place in his mind where no insults could hurt him.

As they moved upstream, Sarah wondered how men arrived at what they became. Sometimes, she observed, there were signs or marks that gave the life tale away. On the morning after they had buried Marano, she had come back to the camp and saw the Negro, Cull, working away at butchering the beast. He had stripped away his shirt, and she saw marks all over his back and chest that had to be the raised scars of repeated whippings. They were old scars and, except for a few on his flanks, had merged together to form an indistinct rubbery mass of flesh. Some of it was dark, and some of it was whiter than her own skin. And after that, she knew about Cull and suddenly was no longer afraid of him.

But she had never known Marano's story, except for what Jojo had said about him—that he was not a priest and that tribes in the region did not believe in his magic or communion with his God. That had troubled her. Even before Marano had saved their lives, she had doubted Jojo's pronouncement on that. Although Marano seldom spoke and had so many funny and strange mannerisms—going off by himself to sleep and almost always eating alone—she knew he was closer to God than any of the priests she had ever seen.

So she understood Cull and sensed that she knew Marano's soul at least, but who was Marte? She had watched him, brazenly even, after her mother had turned away in disgust during their previous encounters with him. She sensed that he delighted in that reaction, the way many men and some women watched for a subtle sign of fear or respect or surprise when they exposed their tattoos or when the soldiers wore their medals or when some of the hired hands who came to the farm showed her notches on their belts. It meant something to many people to be distinguishable, she had concluded. She understood that. The one time she had experimented with makeup, it had given her a sudden hope that she might be pretty after all.

Her mother had cautioned her about that conceit. Emmy never wore makeup and told Sarah that she likely never would have to do so either to be a comely woman, especially here in the Northwest where there were few females, pretty or plain. "The power to manage one's relationships resides inside, not outside," Emmy had told her, and if a person worked on that, practiced finding an unflappable balance while keeping one's senses alert, nothing could ever take that away. Certainly no man, no woman, and not the passing of time or inevitability of infirmity.

But Marte was too obvious, Sarah thought. He was so pathetically transparent in his greed that it would seem almost comical to her if he were not such a very desperate man. She didn't understand him. How did he get the way he was? Somewhere, sometime in his life, probably early on, something horrible must have happened to him, she decided. Instead of scars like the ones Cull had on his back, perhaps they were the ones that grow deep in a person's belly. Marte likely had been defined by the fearful memories of whatever that experience was and had never gotten over it, had never found the courage to go beyond the adaptations he had crafted to survive, so that his cowardice was firmly ensconced into his soul and bearing. As she watched him, Sarah wondered whether Marte's facial definition and his crouched posture were the result of a carry he had initiated at the same time and whether it had just gotten worse with each passing day—that hunch to his back that made him appear even smaller, that forced smile that only came out on the sides of his mouth, a smirk that betrayed his contempt for others. She wondered if people instinctively guarded themselves, prejudicially and unfairly and without provocation, against men like Marte with body and extreme facial characteristics—an unfortunate "physiognomy," as her mother had called it. As exaggerated as Marte's features and expressions were, Sarah concluded that most likely the little man repeatedly had been rejected in his life. She wondered if that distrust by others had compelled Marte into some pathetic pattern of behavior, one in which he would come back over and over for approval from others, just to be pushed away each time—each rejection reaffirming his fears about himself, reinforcing his self-loathing, so that he eventually gave up on himself. Gave up on his soul. Was that what he was about, she wondered? She would have to study him more.

CHAPTER THIRTY-TWO

<><><><><><><><><><><><><><><><><>

ANAH AND JACOB

J acob tried to move, but when he did, the ropes that cinched his hands and feet together behind his back just got tighter, hurting him more. He did not know where he was, and the cold ground seemed to move under him, undulating so that he felt like he would fall from the floor into the sky above. As he opened his eyes, he saw objects lying next to him. They were familiar, but he did not know why. Was that his eagle's beak? His ball of string? He heard barking and curse words and a coarse rattle.

Then his father came to him. He saw his shadow go by, and he held his breath. He wanted to call out for Isaac, but Isaac's shadow just stayed there, behind him, shouting, out of reach. And then his father was gone. And when Jacob opened his eyes again, the things he had seen next to his face were gone too.

Anticipating that Jacob would resist, Klixuatan had drugged the boy. Even then, perhaps because of a tenacious determination to remain in control, Jacob had resisted the drowsy submission that occurred with most captives when given the concoction. Instead, the drug made him delirious and combative. Anah had Klixuatan bind the boy but would not let him increase the dose because he had seen other captives stop breathing when so treated. As he was, powerful as a little defiant wolverine, Jacob was too valuable to waste. So they kept him tightly bound. And after the shaman and his woman tied Jacob's hands and feet behind his back, Anah came to him with something to counter the boy's own magic. They spread out the contents that Jacob had in his pockets the night they had captured him. They had intentionally allowed him to keep these objects, watching for when he became dependent on them as grounding memories—and when they knew the boy was going to them to find reassurance, they stole them away. Then, when they knew he was in the murky depths of his drugged delirium, they laid the objects out again next to his face. Next, they brought out the spirit to break him, if they could.

Anah had skinned and tanned the face and scalp of Isaac and wore it now as a mask. Standing behind the boy, he gestured for Klixuatan to keep the boy turned away. And then he began gesturing with big, bold, sweeping movements—a caricature of what Anah presumed would have been those of the boy's father. The cool leather of the bearded mask and hair formed to his face easily, and as soon as he put it on, Anah felt powerful. He knew that some of the magic of the white tyee was here for him now. He sang and bellowed out white tyee words: "Hey!" "Me!" "You!" "Me-you!" "Mine" "Bastard" "Keep" "Me" "Powder" for several minutes and then stopped, hovering over the boy. Then he backed out of the shelter. Klixuatan watched Jacob that night. He told Anah that Jacob lay motionless but with a rapid pulse that told the shaman they had found the way to control him.

They traveled in four small Kwakiutl canoes carrying their slaves south along the inland coast to the mouth of the river that would bring them east toward the Tsimshian. Except for Jacob, who remained bound, drugged, and hidden, each canoe held two warriors and two captives, all paddling so they moved swiftly. On the second day upriver, they passed the totems of Ksi Amawaal's summer camp, and by the fourth day, they saw signs of Three Spirits where the Tsimshian stayed during the winter. The camp was filled with people, and Anah knew that most were not Tsimshian. Many were drunk. The trading would be easy, he thought. And he wanted to see this Ksi Amawaal and how he got his way.

CHAPTER THIRTY-THREE

◇◇◇◇◇◇◇◇◇◇◇◇◇◇◇◇◇◇

PICKETT

They would attempt to take this easy beach, he had decided. It presented a gentle slope with hard-packed sand. The Brit marines would run up it quickly once landed, so he had to commandeer the highest perch above and, from that promontory, would lob an artillery barrage to impede their progress. Gossip and spies had told him the Brits were indeed preparing for a takeover, ostensibly to protect the rights of the twenty English subjects who lived on the island, but everyone knew that was a Douglas ruse. He wanted San Juan Island for its strategic value, as did the U.S. government. But the Brits would not get it without a stubborn fight from Captain George Pickett. Although he was not to provoke an attack nor fire the first shot, Pickett had his orders. General Harney had dispatched Pickett to hold the island at all costs, even if it meant war between the two nations.

The cold south wind pushed over the long spine that ran from this well-situated parapet to the tip of the island, and even in the murky remains of this day, Pickett could see the entire field of future combat. He saw where the Brit frigates likely would drop anchor, positioning their guns for devastating broadsides against his troops and whatever position he had staked out. Sound carried well in the quiet of the late afternoon, so he imagined he could hear the faint clank of chains and the rubbing squeak of ropes on pulleys as their landing boats made their way down to the water. He heard the shouts of their marine captains ordering the disciplined disposition of their hard men. These would not be children like the Mexican cadets or the peasants conscripted into uniform that he had faced in Veracruz and Churubusco, scurrying backward, brave but undisciplined in their rout. They would be seasoned and mean-hearted Royal Marines. They would most certainly land, take their losses, and determinedly push his equally determined but much smaller company of men down and away from this position. Both sides would suffer. He pulled his slicker closer as the wind bit into his neck. He wished he were in Mexico again.

After an hour of mapping and marking, Pickett called up Lieutenant Henry Martyn Robert from the beach below. "I believe this is the best place to be, Henry. Can your howitzers hit the beach from here?"

Robert, only one year out of West Point, shook his head, then looked again through his field glass to be certain. "No,

Captain. We will likely need to land some of the thirty-two-pounders from the *Massachusetts*. Before it moves away to get out of reach of their frigates. If the reports are correct, they are sending three big ships." Robert was often hesitant but punctilious and almost always right. Pickett simply nodded his head slowly. He knew he would be outgunned and outnumbered. He was determined not to be outdone. As he watched his lieutenant walk back down to the south beach to await the landing of more supplies, Pickett said aloud to himself, "Let them come. We'll make another bloody Bunker Hill of it."

Pickett drifted for a bit. He found himself back in Virginia, where even now, in this early March, color was beginning to show through on crocus-covered afternoons. He saw himself riding down a long lane and paying his respects to some fine young woman and her parents, securing a place and position for himself out of uniform, a dandy gentleman of means. At last. She would be a red-haired filly or a black Irish high-bred dame. He closed his eyes and, for a brief moment, tasted the minted cool juleps that quelled the heaviness of Richmond summer afternoons, so far away from the cutting bite of the whiskey from Frisco that he and so many others in his command resorted to as a meager respite from the cold and boredom of the Northwest. Even here on verdant San Juan, only a few miles by sea from the supplies and excitement of Victoria, he envisioned no relief. So he pulled his slicker even closer and bowed his head slightly to let the light rain fall off the brim of his cap. And then he thought of Emmy Evers.

She was there in his dream, walking right by him, turning her head ever so slightly, telling him she knew he was there, watching her every step and nuanced gesture. His heart began running double-time, and he felt it deeply pounding up through his neck and into his face. He could feel that his face was flushed, and he opened his eyes, and she was there and then she was not. And he wondered if she needed him; he wanted her to need him, but she would never be his and would dismiss him for his arrogant presumptuousness. So, in his dream, she just went on, and he was back in the rain, which was in his shirt and on his back now. It was not a good place to die.

CHAPTER THIRTY-FOUR

KSI AMAWAAL

Ksi Amawaal Sityaawt Gatgyet was widely known to be a very wealthy tyee, so many saw his widely broadcast invitation to this pot-latch as a great opportunity—for the longstanding tradition in the region was that potlatch guests received gifts, and a tyee's wealth and power were measured by how much he gave away. In the entire Northwest, Ksi Amawaal was the most magnanimous of all the chieftains. And when the Ameri-cans spoke of their presidents or the Brits about Victoria, the Tsimshian sneered because their tyee could not be sur-passed in their minds. Thus, clan chiefs arrived from areas as far away as the Queen Charlottes and Nootka, many curious and many envious. To one accustomed to tribal confrontation and protectionism, or to a European concept of ostentation, the wealth displayed by the Tsimshian at Three Spirits was astounding, and most wondered how they had achieved and maintained it. The answer was straightforward. Ksi Amawaal had created a well-maintained, neutral platform for trade, affording protection to everyone who entered. And at this potlatch, every one of the guests brought along goods that might be exchanged in a common market that would develop throughout the encampments. The Tsimshian were healthy, numerous, well armed, and protective of that peace because Ksi Amawaal had long ago shown them how they would prosper if they could act as intermediaries and facilitators rather than as combatants. And observing the disruption to customs and the uniqueness of his tribe's heritage that always ensued after the arrival of even the most well-meaning of interlopers, he tactfully kept missionaries out. Thus, Ksi Amawaal's people had avoided some plagues that had beset tribes closer to the coast. He had also learned to keep his tribe away from the pain of the scourges by listening to gossip from traders and quarantining anyone who appeared for trading during the pestilence. And when the opportunity arose to give cowpox pus to immunize his tribe, he had taken the first inoculation as a demonstration of its power.

Jojo had presented himself as a lone emissary from his father, MaNuitu 'sta, on behalf of Emmy, whom he kept hidden with Sarah, encamped deep in the cedar woods to the north of Three Spirits. When Ksi Amawaal had heard Jojo's eloquent description of Emmy's quest, he understood immediately what he had to do to protect the women and wealth that would come from a skillful negotiation with the Northerners. Alerted by Tsimshian runners who had the ability to move through their woods much faster than canoes traversed up the river, Ksi Amawaal knew the renegades were approaching, dressed as Kwakiutl. He had distaste for headhunters because of the havoc they continued to bring to white victims, and because the Brits and Americans, who could not distinguish one tribe from another, often brought indiscriminate retribution to many tribes, including his own. Ksi Amawaal knew of several misdirected lynchings that had been the consequence of predatory raids on white settlers. The Americans were even less discerning than the Brits, it seemed, so he knew he had to keep his people wary of both white tribes.

And as much as he would have liked to strike the raiders down as they moved in disguise into the Three Spirits, he would need to see the negotiation proceed in order to affect an open trade between the supplicant and the sellers. It was not his way to see blood spilled on Tsimshian rivers because that only dampened profitable exchange and brought bad luck. So Ksi Amawaal waited. And in the hours before the Northerners moved in, he discussed terms with Jojo; negotiated with several other tyees about slaves, tools, and contraband; and prepared his camp for the many feasts that would continue over the next few days.

The whiskey that Marte brought, however, complicated the affair, and by the time Anah arrived, many of the Tsimshian guardians were incapacitated. It would be a very dangerous negotiation.

CHAPTER THIRTY-FIVE

◇◇◇◇◇◇◇◇◇◇◇◇◇◇◇◇◇◇◇◇

ANAH, JOJO, AND KSI AMAWAAL

Jojo took a circuitous route back to the encampment where Emmy and Sarah waited with the gold, doubling back several times to look for tracks other than his own. He found a stranger's footprints on the second pass and knew that someone was following. So he moved far away from Emmy back into the Three Spirits. When he found a small stream, he backtracked in his own footsteps to a heavily branched tree. Using a long, sturdy branch, he vaulted over a bramble thicket and hid in the underbrush waiting for the tracker. He finally showed. It was Cull, making his way carefully, both knives drawn. Jojo watched the huge man tracking in the long afternoon shadows of the forest, his head tilted to the ground with his blind eye turned upward. Jojo held his breath as he watched Cull pass slowly down toward the stream. He knew if he were to have to fight Cull, he would have to move constantly to the man's left blind side, but he also surmised that Cull had survived as long as he had by being very adept at killing with the two long ugly blades and knew many tricks that had surprised many unfortunate men. Jojo cocked his second pistol carefully.

After ten minutes, Cull returned from the stream, inspecting the tracks. He stopped near the tree and looked right up the trunk into the dense foliage to where Jojo had considered hiding. Jojo held his breath. Finally, Cull turned away from the tree, spit, and sheathed his knives. He departed back toward the main camps. Cull had likely given up because, in the waning light, his one eye had not seen the mark from the vaulting pole Jojo had used. But it was evident to Jojo that his tracker was experienced, and he would have to be very careful. He knew Cull would have found him had he tracked earlier in the day. Jojo emerged and followed Cull for a bit to be certain the man was departing. He then swiftly moved back through the woods and found Emmy and Sarah.

"I will need to move you from here now and bring you closer in to Ksi Amawaal," Jojo told Emmy and Sarah back at the camp. "He has agreed to be the negotiator in return for half of the gold. He does not want anything else and does not want any disruption to the potlatch. As soon as he has concluded the negotiation, we are on our own and will need to move to the canoes and leave before Marte or the Northerners find us."

Jojo saw Emmy's and Sarah's concern. "Marte has not told them yet; otherwise, there would have been Haida looking for you with Cull. If I return with Jacob, we will need to move farther upstream and wait for this weather to turn bad again. The Northerners will not expect that. When some time has passed, they should give up, and we will leave the canoes and move by land back to Fort Simpson."

"And if you do not bring him back?" Emmy asked hesitantly.

"Then Ksi Amawaal failed in the negotiations, or he is not among the captives." Jojo looked down, then back up at Emmy.

"Or Jacob is dead."

The words struck Emmy in the gut and her heart at the same time. She recovered her composure and jutted her chin forward to contain a desperate urge to weep. Then, with a bravado, she said, "And if he is there and Ksi Amawaal fails in his negotiations. Then what?"

The intensity of her stare must have given her away, for Jojo shook his head. "Following them would be very dangerous, Mrs. Evers. They will be looking for us anyway, and we could fall right into their hands."

Their gazes locked, hers determined and his beseeching. Finally, Jojo sighed and then nodded. "If he is there, I will do my best to win him back for you."

On the next morning, it began to rain hard, so many people stayed inside their shelters and longhouses. That continued most of the day, and by midafternoon, many were drunk on Marte's liquor. Shortly before dark, Anah, heralded by Klixuatan and leading the tethered gifts of two adolescent slaves, presented himself as "Taxcilsi' Na," a Kwakiutl tyee, to the Tsimshian chieftain.

Ksi Amawaal's younger brother received them and waved the entourage into the longhouse. Anah seemed stunned by the wealth displayed—beautiful furs and sculptures, delicately stitched wall hangings, abundant food, and many beautiful metal hammerings. A few minutes later, Ksi Amawaal, bedecked in a multicolored and feathered ceremonial gown, entered from a side portal accompanied by five other tyees from Tsimshian and Bella Coola clans, all of whom were also beautifully dressed. By comparison, the Northerners had only their tattoos and shell labrets with simple clothing designed for rapid travel. Ksi Amawaal bade them all to sit facing each other on long ornately carved and sanded cedar plank benches. In the murkiness of the smoke-filled room, Anah and Ksi Amawaal measured each other. Neither blinked. Then Klixuatan stepped forward and addressed Ksi Amawaal in the Tsimshian dialect.

Jojo, who had entered with Ksi Amawaal's group but kept to the rear of the contingent, studied Anah's entourage intently. The shaman's pronunciation and accent were so bad that it made Jojo smile at his clumsiness. It almost made him forget, for a moment, that the old man, like everyone in his group, was a brutal killer.

"Mighty Ksi Sityaawt Amawaal, I speak for my leader, Tax-cilsi' Na, in giving you praise for being a powerful tyee. He gives you these strong young women as a tribute to you and your family and your daughter who is joining you with the Bella Coola." As Jojo watched, it was apparent that Anah did not understand everything his shaman was saying, but Ksi Amawaal did. He bowed to Anah, and Anah bowed slightly back. Klixuatan went on. "We are here to trade, with your blessing, with other tyees or Tsimshian and Bella Coola who might have need," Klixuatan indicated the slaves, "for what we bring."

Ksi Amawaal nodded, then looked toward the door. Klixu-atan turned to one of the younger men in the Northerners' company who stepped outside and then reentered with eight tethered captives. Jacob was the last to be led in the door. Jojo recognized him immediately and saw that Ksi Amawaal did as well.

The negotiation proceeded just as Jojo had predicted to Emmy. For all eight of the captives, Ksi Amawaal first offered a variety of gifts, including the items that Emmy and Jojo had ferried up the river. Klixuatan, without conferring with Anah, immediately rejected that offer. Then Ksi Amawaal conferred with his younger brother and two of the Tsimshian tyees. He turned back to Anah and offered the equivalent of two hundred U.S. gold dollars for all the captives. That caused Klixuatan to pause and confer with Anah, who held back even then, rejecting the offer. Ksi Amawaal feigned dis-appointment but again consulted with his tyees. He doubled the price. Klixuatan turned to Anah and held up four fingers. Anah looked over his slaves and shook his head again.

On cue, Ksi Amawaal turned one more time to his conferees, then, after a brief discussion, back to Klixuatan. He pointed to Jacob and held up four fingers. Jojo held his breath during the long pause that ensued. He recognized that when Anah and Klixuatan saw this offer, they knew immediately that Ksi Amawaal had perceived the value of Jacob. Jojo expected more haggling, but instead the Northerners shook their heads, stood up, and walked out of the negotiation, taking their captives with them.

Jojo had not anticipated this reaction. Did Anah and Klixuatan believe Jacob had some special magic? Unfortunately, Ksi Amawaal's bargaining had confirmed their fears. Perhaps they believed selling Jacob would confer to someone else a power they did not yet understand but needed to harness.

Anah made his way back to his encampment, apoplectic at the encounter. Screaming loudly to Klixuatan, he instructed the shaman to bind Jacob again and then attempt to sell the remaining captives for as much gold as he could get from whomever was willing in the entire encampment. They would depart when the shaman had traded enough to purchase the weapons and cannons Anah needed for the coming raiding season. As he watched Klixuatan fumble with Jacob's ropes, he began bellowing at the sky.

And it was in this state of distraught agitation that Rene Marte and Eben Cull found Anah. Marte had held back on approaching the Northerners, anticipating that if he could not succeed in bringing Emmy and Sarah to them before the negotiation, he would be better served by tracking Emmy afterward and returning with three captives instead of two. Unfortunately for Marte, he did not understand the relationship between Anah and Jacob and thus had not expected the negotiation to fail. When Marte told Anah he had traveled with Jojo and Emmy and knew they were the negotiators behind Ksi Amawaal's ploy, Anah became silent. He started chanting to himself. Klixuatan and the other Northerners quietly backed away behind Marte. And then, in one swift motion, Anah drew his knife and leaped high at Cull, plunging his blade deeply into the man's neck and downward into his chest. As Cull collapsed, Anah whirled and pulled his blade across Marte's throat. Marte fell across Cull. Wiping his knife on Marte's back, Anah stood and then spit on their bodies.

Later that afternoon, Klixuatan returned with gold and other goods he had traded in exchange for the seven other captives. They struck camp and began preparations to move westward.

Safely hidden, Jojo was watching.

CHAPTER THIRTY-SIX

◇◇◇◇◇◇◇◇◇◇◇◇◇◇◇◇◇◇◇

JOJO

They followed the four canoes from a safe distance, and fortunately, because the rain was constant now, visibility upstream was limited. By the way the Northerners moved swiftly downstream, Jojo knew they were eager to depart the Tsimshian stronghold before anyone discovered who they really were. He knew Anah likely had what he wanted and almost certainly had assumed that Ksi Amawaal would behave as he, Anah, would have behaved himself, keeping the gold and killing the whites.

The river was moving swiftly now, and the ice had all but melted. They soon passed the shoal where they had escaped the bear. Thirty miles farther downstream, Jojo pulled them ashore to rest. He moved into the woods and, a few miles downstream, found the Northerners encamped, all nine in their party huddled around one fire. Jojo watched for over an hour until all the men had moved under the canoes to sleep.

"I can see Jacob," he told Emmy and Sarah on his return. "There are no other captives. We will need to follow them for another day. They are moving fast, and they will be close to Fort Simpson in less than two days. Tomorrow night we will move ahead past them and get soldiers from the fort to intercept them."

"What if they move inland to avoid the fort?" asked Emmy hesitantly. "We will miss them then." Jojo nodded, considering the pain he heard in Emmy's voice. He did not have an answer for her.

The next morning they moved slowly down the stream, until Jojo pulled them aside half a mile above the Haida camp and reconnoitered again. Inspecting the ashes left from the fire on the shore, he knew the raiders had left at least an hour beforehand. They followed again carefully, pulling aside frequently to allow Jojo to scout for a trap and prevent a blunder into Anah's camp. The second night, he returned to Emmy and Sarah after three hours. "They moved downstream much closer to the fort than I thought they would," he told them. "They are preparing to portage their canoes and bypass the fort starting in the morning. That will slow them down, but we do not have time to wait until they are asleep and get to the fort in our canoe. I can get past them to the fort, but it will have to be on foot. Alone. You must wait here with Sarah for me to return."

"And if they leave before you get back?" Emmy asked.

Jojo saw a fierce woman staring intensely at him. "You must stay here," he said. "You must wait for me to return with the soldiers. You will be safe here."

Emmy and Sarah both were crying.

"How is Jacob?" Sarah asked anxiously.

"He is drugged most likely, so he is not moving much. And they have him tethered to a tree," Jojo said. He saw his words were not reassuring to the women. "They are drinking whiskey. Much whiskey. They think they are safe from the Tsimshian. They are very drunk now. They will not be up early. I will be back in time, Missus Evers."

Five minutes later, in the midst of another downpour and in black, cold darkness, Jojo departed for his run to the fort. He ached from the run, and the relentless rain had seeped through his sealskin, penetrating enough that his arms and legs were starting to numb. As he pushed himself quietly through the forest, hoping he was far enough away to skirt the camp with some safety but close enough to the sound of the river to keep his bearings, he thought about the futility of it all if he did not succeed in his run to the fort—if he was too late, if Jacob was dying, or if Jacob was worse off because of the brutality of his experience by Anah. Jojo thought about that ignorant, insane rogue, of Anah's arrogance he had witnessed during the man's negotiation with Ksi Amawaal, and the warrior's cold, smooth murder of Marte and Cull. He thought about how some of the tribes he'd encountered during his travels with his father were savage and uncontrolled, but remembered that MaNuitu 'sta had taught him those tribes that had endured long enough to develop a culture around families had learned ways to control their young men and women. But Anah was such a dominating monster, Jojo surmised that he really had never been controlled in any way by whomever had raised him. No comeuppance, no responsibility to anything other than unbridled passion. There was a failure in that clan's culture—and the very thing that likely had given it strength—the far-reaching terrifying reputation of Anah almost certainly had caused the clan to rot from the inside out. Jojo had seen that by how all of the other men in his party watched Anah move and deferred to his slightest gestures. He was like a mean, rogue bear heading a pack of hungry dogs. Jojo wondered whether Anah was an evil, unkillable, unstoppable spirit.

The rain stopped; he could again hear the audible marks of his movement and realized he was making too much noise. He slowed down, then stopped and listened. No other sounds. It started to rain again, so he ran for several more minutes until he came to the break in the woods where he was certain the Northerners were likely to portage away from the river. He then stopped and listened again, waiting for the rain to quiet. It finally did. Nothing. He was about to move again when he heard it—behind him the muffled snapping of soggy twigs being broken by footsteps. Had he been discovered? He cocked the pistol under his sealskin, unlatched his knife in its sheath, and stopped. Listened. No more sounds from the direction of the encampment, but there definitely was something coming through the brush off to his right. Animal? It was too dark to make out anything. Too much time lost. He had to run now, and as he did so, he felt a bitter terror at the thought of being overtaken by one of the Northerners, possibly Anah himself, and then being cut down short. Failing. He

threw down the pistol—too much to risk on wet powder—
then ran as fast as he could. There would be no time for a
fight, in any case. If a Northerner sentry was pursuing him,
his only chance was to make straight for the fort. And then
he would have to avoid being shot down at the fort's gates
by a sleepy soldier sentry. He wondered if he would survive.
Running harder now, he pulled his knife out of its sheath and
smiled at the irony of it all.

CHAPTER THIRTY-SEVEN

◇◇◇◇◇◇◇◇◇◇◇◇◇◇◇◇◇◇◇◇◇◇◇

EMMY AND ANAH

Emmy was exhausted. Still, she lay awake most of the night, waiting. When she did nod off, she drifted into the day and saw herself facing the Northerners, spiriting Jacob away from them. Then she and Isaac were together again. He was disagreeing with where they should go with Jacob, and their son was confused, and she heard the Northerners coming back to her home on Whidbey again. This time she told Isaac, who was hurt, to lie down and hide because she would take care of Jacob. Then the Northerners were pounding at the door again, and Rowdy her dog was trying to help, and the children were safe, and Isaac was safe. She startled awake, regained her bearings, and pulled out Isaac's pocket watch. It was five in the morning, and Jojo had not returned. She could contain herself no longer. She turned to Sarah and gently woke her.

"Sarah, I have to see what is happening to Jacob. You must remain here and wait for Jojo. When he comes, tell him I am moving closer to the Haida. Tell him I will stay close to the river." Sarah understood and nodded.

Emmy smeared mud on her face and hands, pulled her sealskin tightly around her body, cinched the belt on her breeches, and moved downstream. She walked carefully, and by early light, after a one-hour trek along a deer path that bordered the river, she found the camp. All the men were still asleep under the canoes they had moved fifty yards up from the river in preparation to portage past the stretch of river that bordered the fort. Jacob was off to the side, tied to a tree just as Jojo had described. The sight of her boy, alive after three months, overwhelmed Emmy, and she began to weep silently. Then she shook herself and regained her composure, watching for a few more minutes. No one was stirring. They might not awaken for a few more hours, she reasoned. If she could get Jacob before they moved inland and carry him back upstream, they could meet up with Jojo when he returned. If she waited, they might move away into an area where she was certain the soldiers would not follow. Then she would lose Jacob again. Perhaps forever. She waited five more minutes. No sign of Jojo. The warriors still were not stirring. She decided.

Holding her breath and fighting the urge to run directly to her son, Emmy moved in measured steps, knowing that one foot caught on the underbrush might awaken the sleeping captors. She became dizzy and forced herself to stop, take a deep, quiet breath, and let the pounding in her chest subside. With Jacob so close to her, the deliberateness of this caution, with each agonizing, careful step, was punishingly cruel, she thought to herself. And then, when she got close enough to make out his features, she saw he was gagged, uncovered, soaking wet, and slumped over. And for a painful, sinking moment, pushing her hopes down toward the abyss of despair, she saw that Jacob wasn't moving, and she thought she had failed—that her little boy was dead. But then he sighed, and her heart began pounding again.

With contained, focused, and agile movement, Emmy untied him. She kept the gag in his mouth, pulled him up, and threw his small body over her shoulder, noting to herself that he had lost weight since he had been taken. She turned and started to move away from the camp, quickly, so that she almost walked directly into two long stakes jutting out at the river's edge. In the early dawn light breaking through the trees, she saw that the poles had heads on them: Marte and Cull. She shuddered and moved upstream.

Anah had slept fitfully, despite drinking heavily that night. He was not accustomed to whiskey and had always preferred to watch others lose their composure when they drank it. He could take advantage then. But on this night, he had felt anxious and was still angry that Marte had not come to him with information that would have given him an advantage over Ksi Amawaal. He had gold from the sale of his slaves, enough to buy two cannons from the French, who did not accept slaves as currency anymore. They would sell him the weapons willingly because they hated the Brits and knew how much trouble Anah was likely to cause them. Anah had enough for purchase of a good quantity of powder and canistered grapeshot as well, which would devastate any attackers should anyone be foolish enough to fight him.

In a wild stupor from the liquor that night, he had lurched over to the wolverine boy and saw that he was starting to wake up from the drugs that Klixuatan had administered. He was regaining his strength. Anah hollered over to Klixuatan to give the boy another dose, and after the old shaman did so, Anah slipped on the skinned-face mask of Jacob's father. When the drug achieved its hallucinatory effect, Anah would dance and control him again, countering the curse from Isaac's father. But the whiskey and fatigue of the day swept over Anah, and he passed out drunk, still wearing the grisly face of Isaac.

That night he dreamed of his elusive friend, Death. It saw him wearing the powerful mask and stopped. It stopped for him and was turning for him finally, waiting. They would be allies after all.

Anah was the first to waken that morning, and as he stood unsteadily to urinate by the stream, he looked over to where the little wolverine was tethered. He had escaped! And then he heard sounds from the west and saw four longboats of red-coated soldiers moving upriver. The boy had escaped and had

taken his power with him. Hollering an alarm over to Klixuatan, Anah looked to the ground to see where the little wolverine had gone. Despite the rain-soaked ground, he could
make out deep, small footprints moving away from the tethers and down toward the beach. He followed. He would need
the boy. Behind him, he heard Klixuatan groggily waking the
other men and the hollering of the soldiers in the oncoming
boats. They had seen the encampment. Anah moved down to
the river and followed the tracks upstream until he came to a
long stretch of beach. He saw Jacob draped over the shoulder
of what looked like a small man carefully wending his way
over the wide, rock-covered beach.

Emmy had moved as quickly as she could along the low riverbank, avoiding catching herself on exposed tree roots or
twisting her ankles on the large rocks polished round by the
river. She had traversed a half mile when she heard hollering from downriver, several rounds of rifle shots, and then
more hollering. When she turned, in the distance she saw
red-coated soldiers coming ashore, firing into the woods. And
then in the foreground, only fifty yards away, she saw someone walking unsteadily over the smooth stones, following her.
He had a knife drawn. She lay Jacob down and stepped in
front of him to protect him. She would fight the man. But the
man moved directly to Jacob and swung at her with his knife.
Emmy ducked, but the blade sliced through her parka, cutting
into her left shoulder, and she lost her balance and fell.

Pushing herself back up, she heard herself scream, "Get

away from him!" But the man ignored her and stooped down toward her son. As the figure pulled Jacob up and onto his shoulder, he turned and faced her. It was Isaac!

But then Emmy realized it wasn't her husband. The facial mask of Isaac on the man had been pulled tightly back, and she recognized the blond beard and the smooth, straight, silky hair . . . but peering through the eye slits were two evil, hard, obsidian black coals burning straight from hell. This was the specter, the one that had followed her in nightmares for months, the monster that had destroyed her family and changed her life forever. The man raised his knife to Jacob's throat as a warning to Emmy. Then he turned and started to walk away.

Following them, she shouted, "Put him down!" The man kept walking, ignoring her.

As he increased his pace, she shouted again, "Put him down, you bastard!"

He stopped and turned. He stared at her defiantly, and as the lower part of the mask flapped away in the morning wind, Emmy could see him grinning triumphantly. It was a grisly sneer that sent a furious chill deep down into her core and immediately reawakened the encompassing wretched and miserable despair she had suffered at this man's hands. A cold, calm clarity settled onto her that was right and just and perfect for this moment. From less than ten feet away, Emmy drew out the pepperbox. She pulled the trigger and put a bullet squarely through the smiling haunt-mask of Isaac and into the forehead of the savage.

CHAPTER THIRTY-EIGHT

<><><><><><><><><><><><><><><><>

SARAH

Jojo had found Jacob's keepsakes, recovered from Klixuatan's purse, which the savage had used to hex her brother, and had given them to Sarah. Presciently, Sarah had carried several things on this trip that both she and Jacob had shared, and several items that only he would know, little treasures she took out of his trouser pockets and his room from home after the attack: a polished burr, a brass button, a blue-brown steely marble, a spent ticket from their trip to Victoria, several pieces of rounded sand-buffed colored glass. So she added the ones she had brought from home, put all the keepsakes into his hands, and let him finger them one by one. Then she put them all into his pocket and kissed him. When Jacob was returned to her, she cradled him in her arms and told him she would never let him go again. She would take care of him. She would take care of him, her little brother. Could he hear her? Was it too late? Would he ever snuggle with her as he had just a few months before? It would take time to see whether he had been broken; she would work on that, she promised herself.

From these events, Sarah wondered about her own frailty in the face of it all. As strong as she believed herself to be, she foresaw herself over the next few years likely ebbing, doubting from time to time, fraying a bit, surprising the framed image of tranquility she wished to project and protect for herself, like when a stone is dropped into the still pond that a modest person should rely upon as one's only mirror. She would keep guard for that.

She wondered what Jacob would see when looking there with her while waiting for return to soft reflections—if that ever came. She wondered, with all that had occurred, whether he would avoid ever again letting go of the security he would certainly now need, holding on tightly to those precious little things she had found and preserved to help bring him back. And would he come back?

It would take time, she decided. It would take time.

CHAPTER THIRTY-NINE

PICKETT AND EMMY

he shelling from the two Brit frigates began at six o'clock in the morning, just as Pickett had sat down for his breakfast with his staff. The incoming shells, striking the beach five hundred yards east of his camp, reverberated with enough force that coffee mugs flew from their laps and set a few younger officers into a frantic tizzy. Pickett did not lose his composure, however. He had been under fire many times, in Mexico and then from Apache and Kiowa small arms in the badlands of Texas. He had the well-proportioned and measured understanding of danger that can only develop when one is being targeted for death.

He watched the earth spraying up, following each report, and realized immediately that the Brits were simply attempting to intimidate him with their gunnery exercise. So he sat back down, ordered his coffee mug to be refilled, and waited for their range practice to cease. It kept up for an hour, finishing dramatically with a full barrage from the HBMS *Tribune's* and the HBMS *Satellite's* port eight-pounders, all twenty of them. And then he heard the Brit marines' laughter from both ships, rolling across the water as a mocking peripety to their display. It made him furious at the bastards.

The next morning, the barrage started again and continued every day for the next few days, not on the clock but rather on cue with the pouring of his staff's breakfast coffee. Pickett knew they would be tested by the Brits like this in the same manner as he had seen schoolyard bullies taunt smaller children into flight or futile fight. So he waited calmly for three more days, and then, on the fourth, moved his camp with as much solemn dignity as he could display over to the windy south side of the long spit, out of reach from their sneering morning provocation.

It was on that day that he received the note. It was from Mrs. Emmy Evers. She had chartered a passage to the island and was waiting for him twelve miles away at the harbor they called Roche. Would he meet her there the next day to receive a package she wished to personally deliver? He did not sleep that night at all, and, as he lay awake in the tent, blustered about by a heavy southerly gale, he tried to reconstruct his feelings the last time they had seen each other. How was she?

He had read in a Victoria newspaper two months ago that a woman, who had preferred to keep her anonymity, had survived an arduous journey and had succeeded in rescuing her son from a band of vicious Northerner aborigines. Word of that feat had spread down the coast, and he had speculated it could only have been Emmy. But there had been no word from her, and the silence had convinced him he was sadly mistaken. She must have perished. But now that he knew she was alive, he realized it could only have been her! What would she say? What would she be like? He needed to know. He was up at five the next morning and waited for another cannonade. But none came. So at nine o'clock, containing himself no longer, he ordered his mount and rode west unaccompanied by an orderly.

Upon her arrival, Emmy had booked lodging for one day with an American couple who maintained a small house overlooking a protected cove shared by two other families, one British and the other loyal to neither country. As she awaited Pickett, she wondered if he would respond, and when she found herself hoping, she thought again about the propriety of this encounter, curious as to what family and friends might think. But she reminded herself that she had finally decided she did not really care what anyone thought. Something had compulsively drawn her to Pickett, and she still did not know what it was. She needed his counsel, she told herself. And she wanted to finish a conversation that had been initiated on the day they had inspected cattle together on Whidbey.

As she watched Pickett ride up in the distance on his strong gray mare, she thought about the freeing finality of her situation. The week after she had arrived home with Jacob, she had arranged for a quiet ceremony at Isaac's grave. Attended only by Jim Thomas, who dug into the grave, and his wife, Princess Susan, who sang a quiet dirge, Emmy buried Isaac's remains—the mask she had stripped from Anah—with the rest of his poor body. And then it was finished. She stopped dreaming about him that week, and when word came down about the confrontation on San Juan one week later, she decided she would make this trip. And it was nobody's business, she had decided.

Watching him approach, she stepped out onto the porch and walked down to the beach below. She noted that Pickett had the same carry as she had seen the day she met him, slightly self-conscious but with a flair that superseded that flaw. The canter of his horse said something about the rider, revealing a dimension she could not discern from his conversation or in the letter he had first written her. It was a gallant form of communication by him, and it made her heart race, a response reinforced with each toss of his proud mare's head. As he drew up, Pickett paused for a moment, then he swooped down off his horse, pushed his cape aside, slowly dropped his field cap, and bowed deeply in the French manner. When she offered her hand, he pulled it to his lips and kissed it gently.

"My deepest respects for you, Mrs. Evers. My profound, deepest respects and admiration for all that I now know you have endured."

"Thank you, Captain Pickett," she said, swallowing her words out of a desperate need to control herself. "I have attempted to keep these travails from the gossip of the community. It seems I have failed."

"I do not believe you fail in any endeavor, Emmy," he said, smiling but obviously holding himself from saying more.

She nodded, not at his assertion, but in approval of his use of her first name. She plucked up her courage. "May I call you 'Pickett George'?" she asked with a sly smile.

He straightened, and, from his surprised expression, she saw he realized that she knew much about him. "You may, Emmy. You may," he said.

They walked along the beach for hours until the light started to fade, past the pounding surf in a misting rain, and shared with each other what they had endured during the past several months. By comparison, his ordeal was slight, he knew. The stories Emmy conveyed were overwhelming to him, as hardened as he believed himself to be. In fact, a few times he had to turn away lest he show emotions that were not befitting a man of his age.

She asked his counsel about the turmoil that definitely was increasing in the East between the states over slavery. She wondered about whether a confrontation was likely to erupt between the opposing cultures of the North and South, each advocating passionately for its position—one side in favor of imposing a civil solution to the affront to human rights represented by the enslavement of others, the other side defending its rationalized position to preserve an economic infrastructure that had existed for generations. She asked how safe would her children be were she to return with them to her home in Boston? And what would become of him? How would he, as an educated man, place his bets? And how closely tied to his heart would his decisions be?

Pickett did not have an answer for Emmy. He had pondered the same issues about his future but knew he would likely move to where his heart brought him rather than where convenience seduced. He understood the value of passion as an underpinning to everything that ultimately mattered, to everything that defined one's legacy, and to the difference he would or would not make in this life. He looked at the sturdy and beautiful woman who walked beside him and wondered how she might fare and whether she ever could fit into those travels. He had seen much, and as he thought about her, thought of the wiles and courage necessary to survive in a cold, brutal world, he sensed she would endure and likely flourish. She did not need to be protected, and that realization was a comfort and a disappointment to him all at once, bred as he was to believe that being a hero and rescuer was a noble reason for a man's existence and ample enough foundation for a durable love. He did not have an answer for Emmy.

And he was duty bound for now, so hoping for a future with her in any case would be far-fetched and out of his control. So he was silent, and they walked on.

They stayed together there for the balance of the day and then, on the next day, she returned home. On the morning she left, she presented him with the inlaid box that contained his Belgian Mariette six-barrel pepperbox. It was the last time they saw each other.

CHAPTER FORTY

◇◇◇◇◇◇◇◇◇◇◇◇◇◇◇◇◇◇◇◇◇

EMMY

Emmy looked over the rail, looked at the dock below, and then up at Port Townsend, framed by the deep green forests and blue mountaintops of the Olympics. It was warming now, and enough blue patched through the clouds that, it seemed, she saw the land again in a way she had not since the time she had first arrived so many years ago. She would round the Horn again, going against every vow she had made after that first awful journey, and present her children to her family for the first time.

She wondered whether she would ever return again, here where so much was buried now. Isaac was finally at rest, she knew. His soul finally had moved on.

She looked north and thought of George Pickett again. She had heard he had faced down the Brits up on the San Juan and that General Winfield Scott himself had trekked across the Panama isthmus to take over and attend to the final treaty. She wondered how Pickett George would fare in a world of men who thought themselves and their business and causes so important. She had written to him once since her visit there. She wished that noble, sad man great luck in this desperate world.

She thought of Jojo and how brave he had been and how grateful he was to receive from her the ability to read. She believed the leverage such a commodity would provide to him was a fair exchange after all. They found his father, MaNuitu 'sta, gravely ill when they returned, but Jojo had been able to read to him before the old tyee died. She knew she had fulfilled an important promise to MaNuitu 'sta—for the time being, the best she could do in return for all he had done.

Would she ever return here? Would her children come back here someday, to this raw and savage land that seduced one with its beauty but tested one so severely with its moodiness? The terrible changes in seasons constantly reminded her she was alive but mortal, she had decided. She wondered what it would be like if she were to live in a climate where the seasons were less dramatic. Would that cause her to become tepid and complacent and forget about death? Would that be fair?

And what should she tell her family in Boston? What should she write about her own thoughts and memories? What could she preserve for others that would be an adequate mark for her time, her family's suffering, and everything she felt so deeply? All so real and yet all so unreal. All so painful and all so much at rest now. All at rest . . . and with her duty done. Could she ever come back? Could she ever will herself into that time and make things right somehow, the way they had been before Isaac had been killed? So much was buried here. But so many people were arriving now and building over it all that soon it would not matter what rested here from before.

The reality, she knew, as she reflected on her journey here in this big Northwest, is that our finite time here does not allow us to really go back. The biographies and autobiographies, based on the exploration and interpretation of the notes we have saved and the markings shaken loose from the corners where we have tucked them, most often stay unwritten. Thus, the memories and mementos become encumbrances, if not for us, then for the family, friends, and strangers who must clean up afterward. Instead of them being loving presences with fragrances that grace a room, they become pale pieces of paper with words that no longer echo and move mountains and souls. A pity, she thought. But there was still much to see in this life, and that was good.

She would accept that and move on.

◇◇◇◇◇◇◇◇◇◇◇◇◇◇◇◇◇◇◇◇◇

ISAAC, ANAH

Out of darkness . . . and suddenly he was a leaf on the porch pushed across with the yellow and orange ones, blowing across the stoop of this home that was his. It was west to east, this wind from the strait below, and he couldn't be angry with it as he had in the past for pushing him so, because then he was part of it, this wind. Now he finally understood why it had howled when it found tunnels to whistle itself through. He finally understood that it was a joyous cry because the sound gave him a voice that lasted for just a bit as he buffeted about. He found a place, a little tube from a broken bottle stem, and he dove into it, and its glass walls vibrated, and he heard the echo of the yearning whistle, a whoop and a warning, and as he swirled up out of it, he was borne up again and he was flying high above what had been his home but no longer was. And as he swooped above, he was in control, and by leaning to the right, he soared high above the beachhead and homestead and saw it all, with its time passing below, all the elements waiting for their time to fly like him.

He hovered out above the sliver-moon bay, above the ship with sails that was empty, and as he landed on its mossy deck, he found scratches on the walls left by sad creatures in sad pain. He hopped along the gangway and saw the drops of blood, long dried and faded, that told some other tale that he could no longer remember. In an empty, dusty room below, next to a broken chair, he found a globe of glass, and inside was a snowing scene with a bright shiny pin inside. He picked it up in his beak and pushed himself aloft and out above the dead ship. He took himself to a shoreline where he saw a rocky beach to drop his prize, burst it, and get the shiny pin. And as he let go, as he had always done so cleverly, something came from out of nowhere, and his catch was gone. And he was wandering again, and his shore and ship and moon were gone, and he was in darkness without a bearing.

AUTHOR'S NOTE

◇◇◇◇◇◇◇◇◇◇◇◇◇◇◇◇◇◇◇◇◇

Widow Walk is a historical adventure novel depicting real and fictionalized characters and events.

Isaac Ebey, recreated in *Widow Walk* as Isaac Evers, was a prominent citizen and pioneer of the mid-nineteenth century Pacific Northwest. Like so many other enterprising speculators in this turbulent era, he had migrated with his skills to California in search of quick fortune. He found none. Luckless and frustrated, he turned his entrepreneurial hopes to the Oregon territory. When he arrived in the Puget Sound area in 1850, fewer than 1500 white settlers had settled there. With the discovery of gold on the Fraser River in 1858 all of that changed and a great booming migration began, with settlers moving northward by ship into the region from California and overland from the Midwest. After surveying areas like Lake Washington and Whidbey Island, Ebey energized that migration by writing effusive letters to friends and relatives, encouraging them to emigrate "before the good land is all taken." He participated in the establishment of the territorial government in the southern area of Puget Sound and suggested the name "Olympia" for the Tumwater location that subsequently became the territorial capitol. In his duties as a tax collector and regional magistrate, he traveled extensively and immediately understood the importance of San Juan Island as a strategic opportunity for the United States. His exhortations to the territorial government recommending it move settlers onto San Juan Island helped the United States' case for its claim to the island against Britain. Greatly disturbed by the constant threat of predation and conflict, in 1856 he outfitted a company of volunteers to fight in the Indian wars in Eastern Washington and was widely praised for his help in subduing native tribes.

The fatal cannonade by the U.S. Massachusetts on encamped natives at Port Gamble is thought to have provoked the attack on Ebey and his family and his brutal murder and beheading by Northerners prompted the settlers and military in the region to intensify their precautions as well as their rationalization of the random lynching of numerous Native Americans. Sightings of long boats parading Ebey's "tyee" (chieftan) head were reported for weeks afterwards.

Blockhouses still stand, preserved on Whidbey and San Juan Islands attesting to the very real threat of pillage, rape and murder by marauding "Northerners," a term used for miscellaneous clans from indigenous regional native tribes. Although no one single group is likely responsible for the legendary headhunting and slaving, clans from the southern tip of Alaska, western British Columbia and the Queen Charlotte Islands (now called Haida Gwai) were blamed for the most of the late eighteenth the early nineteenth century predation against white settlers and coastal native villages. Many tribes along the coast have stories of conflict with them. Northerner slaving raids, which reputedly savaged the Pacific Coast all the way to northern California, continued until steam-powered vessels replaced much of the naval ships patrolling the region.

Collection of exquisite Haida Argillite carvings and coastal native artistry began in the late sixteenth century and continues to this day.

Anah Nawitka is a composite character, drawn from accounts of several notorious clan leaders with whom the British and Americans contended in their appropriation of "aboriginal" lands. Conflict between the cultures was inevitable, with ample provocation and rationalization for each side's escalation of violent retributive actions. James Douglas, the aggressive and enterprising former Hudson's Bay Company director and first governor of British Columbia, used the same tactics in taking land as had his British counterparts in taking New Zealand aboriginal land. Isaac Stevens, the first Washington territorial Governor, advocated the "extinction" of Native Americans.

Antoine Bill and Rene Marte are composite characters of "Me'tis" - a mixed "breed" of French Canadian and indigenous native parentage, who participated in the exploration, trading, trapping and interpretative needs for the British and American explorers.

Ma'Nauita 'sta, Jojo, and Ksi' Amawal are composite characters of well-known, peaceful entrepreneurial native leaders in the British Columbia region.

Christian missionary work, particularly that of the Jesuits throughout the Pacific Northwest is well documented. The character of Marano Levy is a fictionalized version of a legendary wandering Hebrew man who purportedly travelled the region looking for the lost tribes of Israel.

Captain George Edward Pickett, a West Point graduate and Mexican War hero, was stationed in Bellingham from 1855 to 1860. Ordered by Brigadier General William S. Harney to San Juan Island to pre-empt a British claim to that strategically important territory, Pickett made a show of it and subsequently was described by local journalists as a "fighting gamecock." His comments to the press purportedly were "Let 'em come. We'll make another bloody Bunker Hill of it." His stubborn, well-publicized stand off intensified the confrontation, and for a short while there was wild speculation in the region that another war with the British was imminent. General Winfield Scott was dispatched by President James Buchanon to San Juan Island to deescalate what was being called "The Pig War," because the shooting of a Hudson's Bay official's pet pig by an American settler was the provocation used by Douglas to ostensibly "protect the rights of British citizens" on San Juan. The dispute was finally settled in mediation by Kaiser Wilhelm in 1872.

At the outbreak of the U.S. Civil War, Captain George Pickett resigned his commission in the US Army and returned to his native Virginia to join the Confederate Army where he quickly achieved promotions, fame and notoriety. Major General George Pickett was described posthumously by one of his Union army adversaries, General George McClellan as "the best fighting infantry commander on either side" of the War Between the States.

Emmy is buried in the small cemetery overlooking the fertile Ebey plateau with Isaac and their family.

The site of the massacre remains much as it was in 1858 and many of the Whidbey locals think of it as haunted. On moonlit nights it is purported that the ghost of a woman can be seen walking the plateau."

ACKNOWLEDGMENTS

◇◇◇◇◇◇◇◇◇◇◇◇◇◇◇◇◇◇◇◇

To Allen Hurt and Nick Kazan

For constructive inspiration

To Barbara Bourdeau, Rosemary Ambrosio Bradley, Carmen Bartl, Wayne Bliss, Paul Auerbach, Greg Brown, Shawn Comerford, Joe Curiel, Sandy Diaz, S. P. Hays, Dorbe Holden, Nina Ferrari, Neil Gonzalez, Abby Kitten, Angela LaSalle, Francesca LaSalle, Mo Matthiesen Weber, Dave McClinton, Tina Minnick, Kimberly Moore, Randy Mott, Mary Mulcare, Carey Pelto, Thomas Polizzi, Paul Racey, Sherry Roberts, Tony Roberts, Laura Smith, Sue Taylor, and Theresa Tavernero

For encouragement and comments

And to

Mike Vouri, a Pacific Northwest historian; Washington State Historical Society; and the Native American tribal storytellers of the Pacific Northwest

For historical context and perspective

WIDOW WALK

<><><><><><><><><><><><><><><><><><>

BOOK GUIDE

1. *Widow Walk* has been compared to *Last of the Mohicans* and *Cold Mountain*. How is this story similar to those historical fictional works?

2. Emmy Evers in *Widow Walk* has been compared to other fictional women like Scarlet O'Hara in *Gone With the Wind*. How is Emmy alike and how is she different than Scarlet and other strong female protagonists in literature?

3. In 1858 only five thousand nonnative settlers had moved to the Pacific Northwest. It is estimated that over a hundred times that number of aboriginal ("First Nation") people lived along the coast at that time. Imagine that you were a nonnative settler or a First Nation inhabitant. How would you behave if you saw strangers arrive at your home?

4. Conflict between the new settlers and First Nation peoples was inevitable and sometimes became violent. Expansion of population into new territories was impor- tant to both the US and Britain. Was the "jingoism," as manifested in the mid-nineteenth century American and European history, beneficial or destructive?

5. What was the impact of the Christian missionaries in Pacific Northwest history?

6. The responses of the white governments and native peoples to the massacres as depicted in *Widow Walk* were frequently harsh. In your opinion, were they justified?

7. What is a "potlatch" and why was it important to the Pacific Northwest First Nation tribes? Why did the white governments and missionary eventually outlaw the potlatch? How is the potlatch in the twentieth and twenty-first centuries different than the tradition as originally celebrated? Is this good or bad?

8. What is a totem and what is its importance to Pacific Northwest First Nations peoples? What is the signifi- cance of the animals depicted in *Widow Walk*? Who is Raven God in Pacific Northwest native lore? Are there similarities between these archetypes and those found in other cultures?

9. Imagine your family is expecting the birth of another child during the mid-nineteenth century in Pacific Northwest. How would you prepare for this event? Why did so many women die during and after childbirth in the nineteenth and early twentieth centuries?

10. Given the predatory actions of Anah against white settlers and other tribes as depicted in *Widow Walk*, he can be interpreted as sociopathic. How dependent on a society's economy is its management of sociopathic behavior?

READY FOR THE NEXT CHAPTER?

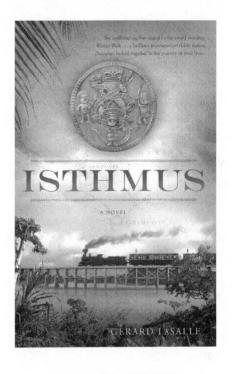

◇◇◇◇◇◇◇◇◇◇◇◇◇◇◇◇◇◇◇◇◇◇

The award-winning *Widow Walk Saga* continues with the second book in the series *Isthmus*. Emmy's family traverse a hostile terrain on the new Panama isthmus railroad, the most modern transportation in the world. A revolutionary ride through the jungle. An inconvenient assault. A run for their lives.

Start reading today at **www.GerardLaSalle.com**.

Made in the USA
Middletown, DE
26 April 2015